Please return on or before the latest date above.
You can renew online at *www.kent.gov.uk/libs*
or by telephone 08458 247 200

CUSTOMER SERVICE EXCELLENCE

Libraries & Archives

00884\DTP\RN\07.07   LIB 7

The Missing Millionaire

DANI SINCLAIR

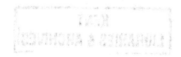

MILLS & BOON

First published in Great Britain 2010
Large Print edition 2010
Harlequin Mills & Boon Limited,
Eton House, 18-24 Paradise Road
Richmond, Surrey TW9 1SR

© Patricia A. Gagne 2008

ISBN: 978 0 263 21583 0

Harlequin Mills & Boon policy is to use papers that
are natural, renewable and recyclable products and
made from wood grown in sustainable forests. The
logging and manufacturing process conform to the legal
environmental regulations of the country of origin.

Printed and bound in Great Britain
by CPI Antony Rowe, Chippenham, Wiltshire

DANI SINCLAIR

An avid reader, Dani Sinclair didn't discover romance novels until her mother lent her one when she'd come for a visit. Dani's been hooked on the genre ever since. But she didn't take up writing seriously until her two sons were grown.

Dani lives outside Washington, D.C., a place she's found to be a great source for both intrigue and humour.

For Judy Fitzwater,
with gratitude and friendship.
And as always, for Chip,
Dan, Roger and Barb.

Chapter One

The graceful young woman danced her way to the table and performed an indecent bump and grind right before his eyes. Slowly, in time to the hot beat of the driving music, the blonde slipped the first button from its hole on her whiter than white shirt and tossed her head. A thick cascade of pale wheat hair shimmered under the light.

"Hasn't anyone told these women sun worship is out?" Harrison Trent murmured softly.

Artie Van Wheeler chortled in response. "You have to admit that getup wouldn't look the same against bleached white skin."

While their friends cheered and egged the dancer on, the woman continued to strip, up close and personal. Harrison took a tentative swallow from his glass and let his gaze skim over the lavishly decorated room and the tacky signs that wished the groom-to-be a lot of things, most of them humorous, all of them wicked. Artie and Carter Hughes had gone to great lengths to decorate the party room. Helium-filled condoms hung from crepe paper festooned with naked body parts. Harrison didn't want to know where his friends had found that particular crepe paper. The ice sculptures on either end of the bar were also graphic and drew Harrison's gaze right to where it had no business returning.

Tall and slender enough to pass for a man in her black tuxedo, with a cap of short, dark, unruly hair and elfin features, the bartender had drawn his attention the moment he walked into the room. He was struck by the way she surveyed the crowd with an odd intensity. Her eyes were never still and he found himself wondering what color they were.

Now, there was a woman who might be worth watching disrobe, music optional. Unlike those of the mostly naked dancers circulating in the room, the form beneath that tuxedo made him think of a sleek predator.

He watched her bend to mix another drink. She moved with an economy of motion that was unconscious grace. Maybe she was a dancer after all. Unlike his much shorter bride-to-be, she was a woman he'd be able to dance cheek to cheek with if he wanted. And he shouldn't be thinking along those lines.

Harrison forced his attention back to the performers. There were some stunning women in the room, yet something about the bartender kept drawing his gaze back to her.

He found himself watching her from the corner of his eye. Her unruly hair was definitely in need of a good stylist. It looked as if she'd taken scissors to it herself. And from where he was sitting, it appeared as if she wasn't wearing an ounce of makeup. Not that her flawless skin needed any enhancement, but that in itself made her stand out. There was a subtle intensity about her, a hint of something dangerous. He was fascinated.

"I've got to say, she is gorgeous," Artie murmured. "And she certainly can move those hips."

Harrison yanked his attention back to the enthusiastic dancer who, even as he watched, reached for the zipper of those tight, white leather shorts that barely covered a thing. The button at her tiny waist was already undone. Smooth golden skin trailed suggestively downward, yet he couldn't summon any enthusiasm. He probably wouldn't have been able to even if she'd been the first dancer of the evening.

His temples were starting to throb in time to the music and his vision was beginning to blur. He would have blamed this on the alcohol, but he was still on his first glass despite repeated toasts.

Harrison lifted the heavy Waterford crystal and took a more generous swallow of the tepid liquid. Maybe if he finished the drink he could get up and find out if the bartender was as interesting up close as she was from a distance. He wondered what sort of voice went with that face and if her eyes were dark blue or brown like his own.

The flying shorts that whistled past his head and into the cheering crowd brought his attention back to the dancer. She was really up close now and a little too personal for his taste. She was also down to a miniscule G-string and a couple of tasseled pasties. The smile plastered on her too-red lips was directed right at him.

At Artie's nudge, Harrison pasted an answering smile on his own lips. After all, the groom and his best man were the center of attention tonight even if Harrison didn't want to think about the coming wedding. What would this roomful of well-meaning friends say if they knew the bride-to-be was showing signs of second thoughts and was pregnant with another man's child?

Were they making a mistake?

He forced the thought aside. From the start, Zoe had been more than a hired assistant. Liking and respect had quickly matured into the sort of friendship that generally took years to form. He trusted Zoe the way he trusted Artie and Carter. They were family to him, and family took care of their own.

It was bad enough that Zoe had watched her baby's father shot down in front of her, but now his killer wanted her dead as well. Harrison was not going to let that happen. By marrying Zoe, he could offer her the protection of his wealth and see to it that her child was not born a bastard as he had been. It was the right thing to do. The only thing to do.

The dancer reached out, lifted his glass from the table and turned it to place her lips exactly where his had been a moment before. She took a small sip and smiled seductively. The room cheered as she bent down, tassels shaking, and kissed his forehead.

He managed a wink and she giggled.

The other men called out suggestions. Even Carter unbent from his formidable lawyer persona to look mildly amused. Harrison kept his smile pasted in place and wished for a speedy end to the evening. The dancer turned her attention to Artie. He dutifully reached out to put more money in her G-string. In the process, her elbow caught Harrison's glass and it tipped. The liquid splashed across the table.

One of the scantily clad servers appeared to mop up the damage, fluttering eyelashes that nature had never designed. His gaze drifted to the bar. He had the distinct impression that his bartender was disgusted. Their gazes locked briefly in sympathetic accord before she turned away and handed a new drink to one of the servers. The woman promptly headed in his direction.

Harrison abruptly realized what he should

have known from the start. The woman wasn't merely a bartender. He'd stake good money she was one of Artie's rent-a-cops for the evening. That explained her constant scrutiny of the crowd. The only way security could mingle was to pose as one of the bartenders, waiters or dancers. Of that group, only the bartenders and Artie's live-in housekeeper were fully clothed.

Harrison surveyed the room with a more jaundiced eye before gazing at his new drink with disfavor. What did Artie think was going to happen in here? With all his little security gadgets, his place was like Fort Knox.

A glance toward the bar found the dark-haired bartender intently focused on him with an expression he couldn't decipher. He picked up the drink, tipped it in her direction and pretended to take a sip. She inclined her head in acknowledgment and he immediately lowered the untouched glass to the table. When he looked back a few minutes later, she was gone.

Harrison straightened up. The blond dancer

shook a tassel against his ear. Whatever had been holding the tassel in place lost the battle. He hoped he hadn't sighed out loud.

THE TRILLING OF HIS CELL PHONE pulled Harrison from a dream he couldn't remember. More asleep than awake, he swiped at the insect biting his forearm as he tried to roll over to answer the summons. A muffled curse brought him all the way out of sleep.

An ominous shadow loomed over him, backlit by the light flooding in through the open bedroom door, which he clearly remembered closing. He had a second to make out an indistinct outline before a slim, firm hand clamped over his mouth.

"Be quiet," a silken voice urged. "I'm not going to hurt you."

Harrison threw his weight against the body behind that hand even as his cell phone stopped its musical demand.

"Help me!" the feminine voice demanded.

A second person surged forward, cursing the cell phone and the person on the other end. There was a crunch followed by a harsh expletive as the other person grabbed for his legs. Together, they attempted to press him into the mattress.

"I stepped on the damn syringe and broke it!"

"Never mind. Hold him down."

A knot of fear spiked through him. A syringe, not an insect. Even as he registered that both of his attackers were women, he realized they were making no attempt at silence. Something was very wrong. Numbness was taking hold of his extremities. A dark cloud fogged the edges of his mind.

They'd drugged him!

Panic lent him strength despite the weakness flooding his body. He swung his hands at the shadowy shape nearest his head, feeling only momentary satisfaction as he connected. The woman inhaled sharply, but didn't release him. She fell across his torso, effectively blocking him from taking another swing.

Harrison bucked hard. His legs tangled in the thin blanket and sheet. Wooziness spread with devastating speed.

"Stop fighting!" the woman ordered. "We're not going to hurt you!"

"Drugged!"

"Yes. Give it a minute."

He swore, struggling all the harder, fighting the drunken feeling as much as his captivity.

"How long does this stuff take?" the second voice demanded.

"I don't know. Hold him still!"

The first woman sprawled across his bare chest as the sheet and blanket slipped lower. She was trying to use her weight to pin him to the bed. Her skin gave off the faintest scent of coconuts. He shook his muzzy head, bucking harder. One bare leg came free of the tangled sheets. The second woman let go as he managed to kick her in the face.

"Ow!"

More curses filled the room as she swore viciously. Her light-colored hair swung about her face.

"That hurt! He'd better not have left a bruise. I've got a job on Monday."

"Will you hold him still!"

"I'm trying."

With the last of his fading strength, Harrison jerked his body hard to the side and rolled. He carried the first woman and the sheets and blanket to the floor with them. They bounced off the nightstand, sending the lamp and alarm clock crashing down on top of them. His head connected sharply with the corner of the night-stand. For just a second Harrison thought he was going to black out.

Neither moved for a stunned instant. He'd landed on top of the woman, one hand resting on a soft, firm breast beneath the thin material of her black jacket.

As their gazes locked he recognized her—the bartender from the party. She squirmed against his length. Unaccountably aroused, he squeezed the breast beneath his hand. She burst into motion, shoving at him with all her might. The second woman came around the bed and grabbed his shoulders from behind. He twisted to fight with her and the world blurred and faded away.

"JAMIE! Are you okay?"

Jamie Bellman struggled out from under the very naked, partially aroused man and rubbed at the aching spot where the lamp had cracked her head. Her fingers came away dry. No blood, but it hurt like the dickens.

"Calm down, Trent," Elaine was saying, "or we'll have to hurt you."

Harrison Trent didn't answer.

"Trent?"

"The drug kicked in," Jamie told her, taking in his vacant expression.

"About time."

"Help me get him to his feet. We'll have to get some clothes on him."

"Yeah. Kind of a shame, though, huh?"

Embarrassed by the way Elaine was ogling his nudity, Jamie tried not to stare as well. Silently, she had to agree that Harrison Trent was an extremely attractive man, dressed or not. Even if he hadn't been the focus of tonight's assignment, she would have found it difficult not to watch him.

He swayed unsteadily when they got him to his feet. Jamie looked around for the clothing he'd worn earlier. The tailored suit and conservative hairstyle seemed like so much camouflage on a man she sensed kept a more primitive side reined in tightly.

"Over there."

An expensive-looking suitcase lay open on a stand near the wall. Elaine gathered up clothes while Jamie continued to support him. He swayed, features slack, eyes mostly shut. Even drugged the man was too good looking for comfort, and potentially dangerous.

She knocked Elaine's arm aside when the

other woman dumped his clothes on the bed and ran a caressing hand down his bare chest.

"Knock it off. We're running late."

Angry, and ashamed of Elaine's actions, Jamie elbowed the woman out of the way.

Elaine merely laughed. "Prude. Can he dress himself?"

Jamie shrugged, wishing she was anywhere but here. "We'll find out."

He could, but his movements were sluggish and uncoordinated. He kept trying to lie back down or touch her.

"Soft," he murmured as his fingers brushed the side of her face.

"Yes. Hold still while I zip your pants." It was entirely too intimate and she hated that Elaine continued leering.

"Quiet drunk," Elaine commented. "Two of us, and mostly all he wants to do is sleep."

"Be grateful. Get his suit jacket," Jamie ordered.

"What for? Is this a formal kidnapping? It has to be eighty degrees outside."

"And the van and the house are air-conditioned and it's supposed to rain tomorrow. You want to stand around and waste time discussing this? We need to hurry. Van Wheeler could be back any minute."

Elaine scowled but headed for the closet. Thinking of Artie Van Wheeler added speed to Jamie's own actions. Neither of the large men was someone she wanted to tangle with. She should have listened to her instincts and refused to come.

Jamie found Trent's shoes and got him to sit on the edge of the bed without falling over. They should have been at the safe house by now. Instead they'd been caught flat by the host's unexpected late-night visitor.

The original plan had been to slip Trent the drug at the party. When he became aroused, Elaine would let him lead her from the room for what everyone would think was a private tryst. Unfortunately, their victim hadn't been in the mood to drink. Even after Elaine deliberately spilled the contents of the weak drink he'd been nursing all night, Trent hadn't taken more than a sip from the new glass Jamie had doctored.

As far as Jamie was concerned, it was just as well. She didn't like designer drugs. A person could never be sure how they would react, especially when alcohol was added to the mix. The last thing Jamie wanted was a dead man on her hands.

"You should have slipped Van Wheeler the mickey at the party like you were supposed to."

"Van Wheeler drank too much. And Trent barely drank anything at all," Jamie explained, and wished she hadn't bothered. She didn't care what her companion thought and she didn't owe her any explanations. Mixing drugs and alcohol was never a good idea no matter how safe Tony claimed they would be.

"Yeah? Well, Van Wheeler wasn't so drunk he couldn't get it on after the party."

"For all we know they were just talking."

"Right. Talking."

Ignoring her, Jamie urged Harrison Trent to his feet. He staggered heavily. His hand reached for her face once more as she steadied him.

"Nice," he slurred.

Elaine smirked. "I think he likes you."

Jamie's skin tingled under his touch. "Come on, Mr. Trent." She eased his hand down. "We're going for a ride."

"Tired."

"I know. Me, too. You can sleep in the van."

Kirsten waited for them at the bottom of the steps in the front foyer near the door. The long-haired brunette was tapping her foot when the three of them appeared on the stairs.

"What were you doing up there, having a private party? Come on!"

"Ha. Not with Miss Prude here dictating policy," Elaine complained. She shoved aside a spill of hair as they finished maneuvering him down the flight of stairs.

"Then what took you so long?" Kirsten demanded as they got him out the door.

"He didn't want to come," Elaine told her. "And we had to get him dressed."

"Yeah?"

There was a suggestive smirk in her voice Jamie didn't like.

"He was naked?" Kirsten continued. "I'm really sorry I missed that. He looks prime to me."

"Oh, he is," Elaine agreed.

"Let's get going," Jamie ordered.

"Now you're in a rush? We're home free now, baby. We've got all night."

"And we've used up most of it already," Jamie told her. "Help me get him in the van."

The drive to the farmhouse would be long and her nerves were already frazzled. She had never wanted any part of this. Even if she hadn't known the sort of people Tony had once worked for, Jamie's insides rebelled against the very idea of kidnapping someone.

The problem was, she owed Tony Carillo, and the debt was one she could never hope to repay.

Tony and his wife had never asked Jamie for anything in all the years they'd stood in as her surrogate family. Not once had they made her feel indebted.

That didn't change the fact that she was.

Tony insisted the kidnapping was necessary to save Harrison Trent's life. Beyond that, he wouldn't tell her a thing. Jamie's job was to keep the man safe until noon, when someone would come to the farmhouse and explain everything. After that, Trent would be allowed to leave and no harm done.

She didn't believe in Santa Claus, but Jamie believed in Tony. She swore under her breath. If only she'd picked a different week to come for a visit. She was due to fly back to the coast in two days. This was not how she wanted to spend one of her last evenings. Jamie took her job as a professional bodyguard seriously. She would never forgive Tony if he had lied to her.

With some concern, she studied the man on the backseat beside her. She hadn't gotten much of the drug into him before he'd batted the syringe out of her hand, so there was no telling how long the effects would last. Jamie was thankful he was docile for now. While she was strong and knew some tricks, Harrison Trent was a trimly muscled man who emanated a sense of power even drugged.

And Elaine's leering comments aside, his body went with his face. Trent was incredibly good looking and wealthy enough to be a target for all sorts of people. His bride was going to be very upset come morning.

Debt or no debt, Jamie heartily wished Tony had found someone else for this assignment. On the other hand, if she could prevent Trent from being killed, it was worth doing.

She sighed as the two women in front of her continued their bawdy discussion. No wonder Tony had wanted her in charge. Whether Trent liked it or not, she was going to do her best to guard his ruggedly handsome body until noon.

HARRISON FOUND HIMSELF swaying, groggy and confused as he stood on uneven ground. His back was pressed against a tall vehicle. He stared at the porch of the ratty old house in front of him, trying to make sense of where he was. He felt drunk. But he hadn't drunk much and he never drank to excess. What was wrong with him?

"Come on, Mr. Trent."

He wasn't alone. Three people surrounded him in the humid darkness. Overhead, the sky blazed with stars. What had happened to all the city lights? He shook his head, willing the muzziness to go away, and nearly fell. Where was he? Who were these people? "Wha—?"

A woman took his arm. She was nearly as tall as he was, willowy and surprisingly strong for such a lean woman. He could barely see her features beneath the cap of short dark hair. She guided his shambling steps up the three stairs of the worn old porch.

This wasn't right. He tried to tell her so, but the

protest got all jumbled in his mouth. A second woman moved forward with keys. He reached for the door to hold it open for her and discovered his wrists were taped together. "Wha—?"

"It's okay," the woman holding his arm assured him. "Don't worry about it."

That didn't seem right, either. He thought he should be upset.

The long-haired blonde finished unlocking the door and turned to stroke his cheek. "Hey, handsome, how'd you like to get it on?"

The woman holding his arm knocked the other woman's hand aside. "Leave him alone."

"Hey, I'm not territorial. We can all have some fun."

"Don't touch him." Her voice was cold and filled with warning menace. Her fingers tightened on his arm.

"You aren't in charge here."

"Yes," she told the other woman, "I am. I'm his bodyguard."

"Ha! Nice work if you can get it."

"I did, so back off."

"Chill out. He won't remember any of it."

"But I will."

The words were spaced and deadly calm. Even Harrison's befuddled mind registered the threat and the challenge behind her words and stance.

"Fine, Miss Priss. I guess you want him all to yourself. C'mon, Kirsten, let's go see what they have to drink in this place. Dancing makes me thirsty as well as horny."

"I need my car keys," his bodyguard told the other woman.

"What for?"

For an answer she held out her hand and waited. The brunette with the ponytail fished a set of keys from her pocket and tossed them in his direction. The woman holding his arm caught them out of the air before he could flinch away.

"Where do you suppose Tony found someone like her?" the blonde asked.

If there was an answer, Harrison didn't hear

it. His captor led him down a hall into a small room. A single overhead bulb revealed a neatly made bed that took up most of the available floor space. There was nothing else in the room. Seeing the crisp white cover, he realized how tired he felt. He struggled to free his hands.

"Take it easy, Mr. Trent." She pulled down the cover.

"M'hands."

"It's okay. You're going to be fine. Have a seat."

Even sitting on the side of the bed as she'd instructed felt wrong. His head hurt, and his brain couldn't seem to sort out what was happening.

She pulled off his shoes and set them on an old dresser. A knife appeared in her hand. Her features were unreadable as she slit the tape binding his wrists together and quickly pulled it off, making him wince.

"Sorry. Let's get your jacket off."

There was a sense of déjà vu as she divested him of his suit coat. His movements were oddly disconnected. His hands fumbled and didn't work right, but bit by bit his mind was starting to clear. This was definitely all wrong.

He considered trying to overwhelm her, but his body still felt too uncoordinated. Mentally, he struggled to put the pieces together, getting a jumble of confused images. One thing was clear, he needed to get away from these women.

Reaching for her, he yanked the woman down on top of him. The move caught her unprepared. Together, they collapsed on the wide bed.

"Mr. Trent—"

She struggled and he held on tightly. The feel of her moving against his length aroused him. She smelled good. He'd always liked coconut. And she fit nicely. He covered her lips with his own. They were exquisitely soft.

For a startled instant, she lay over him, quiescent. His body hardened. He wanted her. And that was also wrong.

As if in agreement, she resumed her struggle to pull away.

The keys! He managed to dip into the pocket where he'd seen her put the car keys, making the action part of the silent battle they waged. She pulled away and stood as he rolled on top of the keys, praying she hadn't noticed them fall to the bed. He shifted to cover them as she pulled a roll of duct tape from a different pocket and ordered him to hold out his hands.

"You first." He tried to smile and felt a foolish grin split his face.

Her mouth firmed. "This isn't a game, Mr. Trent."

"It could be."

"Don't make me drug you again."

Drug. She would drug him again. That's why his head was all mush.

"Let me have your hands."

In a moment of clarity, he debated taking her down and decided he didn't have enough dexterity yet. He didn't resist when she reached for his hands.

"Thank you."

She wrapped the duct tape securely around his wrists once more.

"Why?" he asked.

She didn't pretend to misunderstand. "Because like it or not, I was hired as your bodyguard and I intend to be exactly that. By tomorrow afternoon you'll be on your way home. You have my word on it."

That sounded like a vow.

Vows.

He was getting married in the morning. Why was he getting married? He wasn't in love with anyone.

"Try to sleep off the drug's effects, Mr. Trent. You'll feel better when you wake up. If you need something, shout. I'll be right outside the door."

She pulled the lightweight cover over him and turned out the light. In seconds she was gone.

He rested, letting his brain sort through the confusion. Getting the keys from under his body proved awkward, constrained as he was. His coordination was still off and his head throbbed. It wasn't just a dull headache, either. There was a sharp pain in one spot. Had they hit him with something? Why couldn't he remember?

Using the longest key like a blade, he attempted to saw the tape binding his wrists. More than once he dropped the keys and had to fumble for them in the bedding. Each time he paused, afraid she'd hear and come in and take them away.

Somewhere in the house a television played loudly. Twice, one of the other women called out. Once, his bodyguard answered back. She really was outside his door. He froze, afraid she'd come inside and check on him. She didn't, and after a heart-pounding minute he went back to work on the tape.

When it finally parted, he lay there a moment before working it off his wrists. More skin and hair came away with the wad of sticky tape. He was bleeding. He didn't care. He was free and he intended to stay that way.

His thinking was clearer now and he was coldly furious. Someone had made a very bad mistake.

The room was incredibly dark. Little light filtered past the cracks around the door. There didn't appear to be a window. *So much for an easy escape.*

Rubbing at the tender place on the back of his head, he found a raised lump. So they had hit him with something and drugged him to boot. He welcomed the controlled fury that sent adrenaline coursing through him. One way or another, he was getting out of here—even if he had to take on all three of them at once.

They hadn't displayed any weapons other than the knife the woman had used to cut him free. Of course, that didn't mean they weren't armed, but he'd take his chances.

Grabbing his suit coat from the end of the bed, he went to the door and listened hard. No sound. Even the television had fallen silent. Quietly, he searched the room. He was more unsteady on his feet than he liked. He fumbled putting on the shoes he took from the dresser.

While he was feeling more clearheaded by the minute, the room had a tendency to list, especially when he bent over. A quick search proved his cell had been stripped clean of anything he could use as a weapon. He didn't even have his belt. All he had were the keys he'd taken from his jailer.

Well, drunk or drugged, he should be able to take on one woman. Three might prove a challenge, but if they didn't shoot him, he had a chance.

Putting his hand on the door handle, he twisted slowly. The knob turned without a sound. Surprised they hadn't locked him in, he inched the door open, praying it wouldn't squeak. Through the slit he'd made, he peered into the hall. A pillow and blanket lay on the floor. There was no sign of his jailers.

Harrison didn't hesitate. He opened the door, stepped through and closed it behind him as quietly as possible, nearly tripping over the pillow on the floor. He caught himself with a thud against the wall. The sound seemed unbelievably loud in the silence of the house. He paused, but no one shouted. There were dim lights at both ends of the narrow, dark hall. The television had sounded as if it had come from his right, so he went left.

A toilet flushed as he reached the small country kitchen. Footsteps moved rapidly overhead. Harrison didn't waste time searching for a weapon. He went straight to the door, found it unlocked and opened it, half expecting an alarm to sound. Someone was running down the stairs.

He was outside, closing the door at his back. He missed the bottom step and stumbled off the porch, going to his knees. The grass was thick and high, prickling against his hands. He barely noticed. Car keys gripped in his hand, he ran toward the front of the house, heedless of noise.

A large van with tinted windows was parked in front on the rutted dirt-and-gravel strip that served as a driveway. Two smaller vehicles were parked beside it. He debated. She'd said car, hadn't she? He chose the larger sedan, hoping the key would fit. He had a feeling he wouldn't get a second chance.

In the dark, the small lock was invisible. He nearly dropped the key twice before he jammed it into the hole.

She came out of nowhere. One second he was struggling with the lock, the next he was falling to the ground in a tackle the NFL would have approved.

And the house exploded.

Chapter Two

While Harrison was still trying to understand what had happened, the woman leaped to her feet, running toward the blaze. Flames licked at the dry wood with greedy hunger. He climbed to his feet, shocked to see the entire building engulfed in flames. The heat was staggering.

"Elaine! Kirsten!"

He went after her as she attempted to get on the porch. The front window burst outward in a shower of glass. Flames shot through the new opening.

"Get back!" He grabbed her, but she pulled free.

"We have to get them out!"

He was pretty sure it was too late, but his

gaze swept the grounds, lit by the voracious fire. "Is there a ladder?"

"I don't know!"

They ran to the side of the house, seeking another way inside. As if the fire anticipated this, every entrance was thick with dark plumes of smoke as deadly as the flames themselves.

Knowing it was foolish, Harrison used the porch railing to pull himself onto the hot roof. The dry wood framing made the old house a tinderbox. Another window popped, sending more tongues of flame licking up the faded wood siding. Thick, black, noxious smoke filled the air.

"Get down!" the woman yelled.

There was no choice. Harrison swung back down and jumped to the grass. His lungs hurt as he coughed up the smoke he'd tried not to inhale.

She gripped his arm. "We have to go."

"Your friends…"

"They're dead. It's too late." She tugged him

between the van and the car, grabbed the keys from where they dangled in the lock and moved past that car to the smaller one. The smaller car had been protected from the explosion by the other two.

"We have to go," she repeated.

Harrison shook his head. "The fire department—"

"Can only watch it burn." She opened the passenger door.

His head throbbed. He coughed hard. Coughing as well, she practically shoved him down onto the passenger seat. Slamming the door, she raced around to the other side and slid behind the wheel.

"Where's your cell phone?" he asked as the engine roared to life.

"In there." She nodded toward the house.

Surely someone would call. The flames would be visible for miles. Fire lit the surrounding area as it feasted on the house. Without lights, the small car careened dangerously across the choked lawn and down the rutted path that served as a driveway.

Harrison reached for his seat belt as he bounced all around. "Slow down. You're going to wreck."

"No." She swiped the back of her hand across her cheek.

"I'm sorry. Your friends—"

"They weren't. I didn't even like them. But nobody deserves to die like that."

He tried to make sense of her words as she turned the car onto the main road and sped up. "Turn your headlights on. You're going to kill us."

"You don't get it, do you?"

Her fingers gripped the steering wheel fiercely. "Those explosions back there were deliberate, Mr. Trent. Tony lied to me."

There was anguish in that last.

"Someone wanted you dead tonight," she continued.

"No."

She didn't seem to hear his stark protest.

"If you hadn't knocked that syringe aside… If you'd gotten a full dose of the drug, or hadn't escaped when you did…" She stared at the blackness beyond the windshield, never once looking at him. She drew in a shaky breath. "You were supposed to die in there."

Harrison tried to absorb words that made no sense. Nothing that had happened tonight made any sense.

"We all were."

It took him a second to realize she meant they were all supposed to die. "That's crazy."

"I only realized my keys were missing when I went to the bathroom, or I'd have been inside that house along with you. We probably wouldn't have had time to know what happened."

"No one wants to kill me."

"Wrong, Mr. Trent." Bitter acid dripped from every word. "Someone hates you enough to kill anyone in your vicinity."

He wanted to tell her she was insane, but the inferno behind them said otherwise. Thinking was hard, but he knew that fire hadn't been accidental. He'd heard the explosion. More than one. And he'd felt the concussion of the blasts.

Either a gas main had ruptured, or she was right, someone had deliberately blown up the old farmhouse.

His brain felt stuffed with cotton and his head throbbed. He was a businessman. He'd made some enemies, sure, but he prided himself on being ethical. How could he have not known he'd made an enemy willing to commit murder? If only he could think clearly.

"What did you drug me with?"

Her quick glance was troubled. "It's supposed to be a compound similar to Rohypnol."

"Supposed to be?"

Her expression was uncomfortable. She faced straight ahead once more. Her hands continued their death grip on the steering wheel.

"I was told the drug would make you docile and agreeable so we could get you out of the house without an incident."

"You stuck me full of a drug and you don't even know what it is?"

She shifted as though uncomfortable and didn't respond.

Despite the effort it took to keep his rage in check, he strove to keep his voice level. "Why did you kidnap me?"

"To protect you."

Her tone was laced with irony, but there was also anger below the surface. Surprised, he realized she was as furious as he was. "By tying me up in an exploding house?"

"It wasn't supposed to explode."

"How comforting."

"Look, I was asked to guard you until noon. Someone was supposed to explain everything to you then. After that, I was promised that you were going to be set free."

"I hope you got that promise in writing, because you should definitely sue."

Her knuckles whitened on the steering wheel.

"Who was coming to see me?"

"I don't know." The sharpness of her tone didn't disguise a thread of deeper emotion he couldn't identify.

"What *do* you know?"

"We need to get away from here." Her eyes wandered between the empty road in front of them and the rearview mirror that showed the empty stretch behind them.

"Are we being followed?"

"No."

Not yet seemed to be implied. He shifted on his seat and stared at the side mirror. There was nothing to see. "Who promised you I was going to be set free?"

He didn't think she was going to answer, but after a moment, she did. Pain laced her words. "Someone I trusted."

He swallowed a scathing comment. She was angry and afraid, he realized. "Who are you?"

"My name's Jamie. And until noon tomorrow, I'm your bodyguard."

"I don't want a bodyguard."

"Too bad."

Silence filled the car. He studied her stiff posture for several seconds. He thought there was a sheen of moisture in her eyes, but he couldn't be certain.

"Why noon?" And a wave of cold spread through his belly as an answer presented itself. "I'm getting married at eleven. Zoe! They're going after Zoe! Find a pay phone," he commanded.

Fear knifed his thoughts. This wasn't about him. This was about Zoe. She'd been the target of a killer at least twice. Her condo had been ransacked and destroyed. When she refused to move in with him before the wedding, he'd had her move into one of his apartment buildings to protect her. Someone wanted him out of the way so they could strike at her!

BLINKING BACK furious tears, Jamie glanced at the man. She couldn't see his features clearly in the darkness of the car, but she could feel the tension that radiated from his still form. He was more alert and competent with every second. Despite the gun strapped to her ankle, she didn't like the odds if it came down to a struggle. Short of shooting him herself, she wouldn't win a physical contest.

"We need a phone," he repeated angrily.

"Do you see a telephone anywhere?"

"He's going after Zoe."

"Who is?"

"I don't know!"

Jamie shook her head. "*You* were the one in the house that exploded, *not* your bride-to-be." But hadn't she wondered all along if his bride was the intended target?

Except, he was the one they'd tried to incinerate. So why the charade to protect him? And why try to kill him in such a spectacular fashion?

She needed to find a phone more than he did. But the two-lane road was dark. The houses and barns that flanked it were set well back from the street. Tony's people had chosen the location for its remoteness.

"We've got a ways to go yet before we reach the highway," she added.

"Where are we?"

"Southern Virginia." She turned on the car headlights. There had been no sign of pursuit, so likely the explosive devices had been on timers. Yet she couldn't be sure that someone hadn't hung around to trigger those blasts. This was not the time to start taking chances.

Jamie shuddered as she thought about how close an escape they'd just had. She would not believe that Tony had set her up to die. Therefore, someone had lied to him. The person had to know he wouldn't take this lying down. Whoever had set this in motion had a second set of victims in mind. Jamie needed to get to Tony before the killers did.

If only she hadn't panicked and left her cell phone on the sink when she'd discovered her keys missing. Stupid. Now all she could do was race against time and the unknown enemy.

If she was going to have regrets, she should start with the fact that she hadn't followed her instincts from the start and flatly refused Tony the minute he proposed this insanity. But if she hadn't gone along, her mind whispered, it would have been his wife, Carolyn, in that farmhouse tonight.

"As soon as we get to a phone you can drop me off," Trent told her. "I won't tell the police about you."

"Even if I believed that, what part of my being your bodyguard don't you understand?" she snapped. Fear and frustration made her tone sharp. "I agreed to keep you safe until noon and that's exactly what I plan to do."

"I don't need or want a bodyguard."

"Two dead women say otherwise. I'm a professional, Mr. Trent. When I agree to do a job, I see it through."

There was a beat of silence. She could feel him studying her.

"You really are a bodyguard?"

"Licensed, bonded and everything." No need to tell him that was in California, not Virginia.

It was subtle, but she sensed him relax a bit.

"Do you know James Wickliff?"

She shook her head. "No."

"Mark Ramsey? Of Ramsey Incorporated?"

"No."

His tension returned. "I hired Ramsey's firm to guard my fiancée. Wickliff was assigned to Zoe."

"Then she's probably safe enough."

"As safe as I was?"

His bitter words silenced her.

"Were those other two women bodyguards, too?"

"No. What they wanted to do with your body had nothing to do with guarding it. They came with the assignment."

That gave him pause. "Who *are* you working for?"

Jamie debated. What would he say if she told him she suspected a man involved in organized crime had arranged to hire her? Her foster father's former boss had his fingers in any number of pies, though he kept a low profile. His name probably wouldn't mean a thing to someone like Harrison Trent, but if it did, the less said the better.

"I'm working for a friend," she said.

"I'd hate to meet your enemies."

Jamie tensed. "He was set up as much as we were!"

"How do you know?"

"Because I do."

"That's helpful."

She didn't bother to respond.

"This makes no sense," he muttered under his breath.

"What doesn't?" She felt his stare return to her.

"Why would Drake's killer come after me?"

"Who's Drake?"

The silence lengthened. She sent a glance in his direction and found him studying her in the darkness.

"You really don't know, do you?"

"Listen, Mr. Trent, if you know who tried to kill you—"

"I don't. Zoe dated a man named Wayne Drake a couple of times a few months ago. He turned out to be a professional thief. He was gunned down outside a restaurant in D.C. last week."

"So?"

"So Zoe was with Drake when he was killed. The story made headline news."

Jamie could have told him she hadn't been paying attention to the news while she was here. Instead, she sent him a quick glance. "Your fiancée was dating another man a week before your wedding?"

"No! It's complicated."

"Sounds like it. Must have been a big story what with her being engaged to you."

Harrison took a deep breath and exhaled before continuing calmly. She had to give him full marks for control.

"The police don't know if Zoe was the intended victim or Drake was."

"*He's* the one who died," she pointed out.

"But someone had tried to kill her a couple of months earlier."

That was interesting. Jamie tapped the steering wheel with her index finger. Was his bride-to-be involved with Victor DiMarko somehow? DiMarko was reputed to be a good-looking man, if a lot older than Trent's bride must be. On the other hand, if her dead boy-friend had been a thief, maybe he was the con-nection to DiMarko. Or maybe there was no connection whatsoever.

Jamie shook her head. Even if someone had a reason to go after the thief and Trent's fiancée, why try to take out a man like Harrison Trent? He was a millionaire several times over. His murder would stir a hornet's nest of activity for sure.

"Why would Drake's killer come after you?" she asked. "Were you at the restaurant, too?"

"No."

"Then the attempt on your life must be about something else."

"There has to be a connection."

She shook her head. "You're a businessman, Mr. Trent. You've probably ticked off a number of people."

He tensed. "Being a businessman makes me evil?"

"Being a *successful* businessman makes you a target," she corrected. "Did you win any big deals lately? Maybe fire someone with a temper? Step on the wrong toes?" Like Victor DiMarko's? "Start thinking, Mr. Trent, because someone doesn't like you."

"I'm sure a number of people don't like me, but blowing me up is extreme. I don't make that sort of enemy."

"Obviously, you have now."

She drove in silence while he contemplated her words. Abruptly, he pointed toward the windshield. "There's a gas station up ahead. It's closed, but maybe it has a pay phone."

Jamie slowed, considered the spot and then sped up again.

"What are you doing?"

"It's too isolated. We'd be too exposed."

"Stop the car! I have to warn Zoe!"

"And I have to call someone as well, but I'd like us both to survive the experience. We're too close to the house, Mr. Trent. This is the first phone I've seen. I suspect our bomber knows that. I don't want to take the risk."

"I'm willing."

"But you aren't driving."

For a moment she thought he'd make a grab for the steering wheel. Fortunately, he wasn't a fool.

"We'll be on the highway in a couple of minutes. We'll find a place to stop after that."

"If Zoe dies because you wasted time, I'll make it my full-time goal to see you spend the rest of your life in prison."

Her scalp prickled. She didn't doubt him, but she couldn't afford to let his words stop her. "I prefer positive incentives myself."

"I'm not joking."

"Didn't think you were." She forced her voice to remain level as fear churned in her belly. "I don't know who's coming after you. Maybe they will go after your fiancée next. Maybe they already have. What I do know is that they tried to kill you and now they're going to go after my friend because he's the only one who can nail their hides to the barn door."

"Assuming your friend isn't behind the bombing."

"That's a given."

"Is it?"

"Yes."

His voice tightened. "Why should I trust you? You drugged me, kidnapped me and planned to hold me against my will."

Her patience gave out. "That's right, so don't mess with me. I've got nothing to lose. When we find a *safe* pay phone, you can use it after me. In the meantime, be quiet and let me drive."

HARRISON EYED HER with a grudging respect. Her elfin features were determined. He sensed she was telling him the truth as she saw it, but that didn't soothe his impatience to reach Zoe and be sure she was unharmed.

"Is it possible the explosion was meant for you or one of the other two women?" he asked after a few minutes.

Jamie hesitated as if that thought hadn't occurred to her. "Unlikely."

But there was a thread of uncertainty in her tone. The more he considered the idea, the more he liked it. Drake's killer would have no reason to kidnap or kill him, yet if Jamie was telling the truth, someone wanted him to miss his wedding. Why? Drake was dead. Where was the motive?

He squeezed the bridge of his nose, trying to relieve the throbbing pain in his head. The drug had left his mouth cottony dry and his stomach churning. Exhaustion tugged at him, both physical and emotional. As they rocketed down the highway, he wondered what would happen if a cop tried to flag them over. Would she stop? Would she tell the police what had happened?

Would he?

He was used to making snap decisions about people, but Jamie confused him. His initial attraction to her lingered despite what she had done. He couldn't define what it was about her that had intrigued him from the start. But after she sped past the third possible exit ramp, any attraction he might have felt dissolved as he realized she had no intention of stopping.

"We could have found a pay phone at that exit."

"I know. I also know you don't have any change. I dressed you."

Disconcerted, he couldn't decide which was more disturbing, the fact that she was right about the change, or the fact that she'd dressed him. He always slept in the nude.

"Unfortunately, I don't have any change, either," she added.

"You don't need change to dial 911."

She cut him a look. "I have no intention of dialing 911."

That answered the question of what she'd say to the police if they were stopped.

"You could use a credit card."

Her scornful expression deepened.

"Where are we going?"

She said nothing for so long he decided she wasn't going to answer.

"We should get rid of this car," she told him finally.

"What, you don't like the color?"

She ignored his sarcasm. "It's been sitting outside that farmhouse all evening. We're lucky it wasn't rigged to explode, too."

"Now, there's a cheery thought." He shifted at the memory of those horrific explosions.

"It could also have a tracer on it in case one of us did escape."

"Just who do you think is after me?"

"Someone willing to kill four people without remorse."

Put that way, he couldn't think of a thing to say.

JAMIE DEBATED HER OPTIONS. She could steal a car, but the minute she stopped, Trent was apt to take off. Part of her thought that would be just as well, but she couldn't leave him undefended after promising to guard him.

Tony wouldn't be happy when she showed up on his doorstep, but what other option did she have? She wasn't about to ask Harrison Trent if he was involved in organized crime. He might say yes, and she really wanted to like him. He knew how to keep his head. Despite the drug messing with his system, he'd been quick to seize an opportunity when she'd inadvertently presented one. And he'd actually tried to save the other women even though they'd drugged and kidnapped him.

Ruefully, she realized the millionaire was handling the situation better than she was. Jamie didn't want to discover he'd made his money in the same line of work as Tony's former boss.

Whoever was behind the explosions would expect her to go to Tony if they knew she'd survived. But did they know? It all came down to whether the devices had been remotely triggered or on timers.

Her knowledge of bombs was rudimentary at best. Still, it galled her that she had walked into that farmhouse like a sheep last night. Not one of them had thought to check the place over when they returned, and she knew better. Foolishly, her chief concern at the time had been defending Trent's questionable virtue from Kirsten and Elaine. She wasn't altogether sure he'd thank her for that, but he and his friend hadn't ogled the dancers that evening. In fact, Trent had almost looked pained at times.

Except when she'd caught him looking at her.

The memory provoked a tiny shiver. He'd been curious about her. She'd seen it in the way his eyes had followed her. Jamie had been surprised and more than a little flattered. She was blessed with attractive, if average, features, but certainly not the sort that normally drew a man's gaze in a roomful of half-naked women.

And more disturbing, she wasn't immune to him, either. Even now, knowing he was engaged and possibly a member of organized crime, she found him extremely attractive.

Hastily, she shoved the thought aside. She needed to concentrate. She'd seen no sign of pursuit since they'd driven away, but that didn't mean no one was back there. Most likely, the explosives had been on timers. They'd been well planted to effectively block all the main exits. Someone had wanted to make very sure no one escaped that inferno. The chilling thought brought a shiver straight down her spine. Would she have found the devices if she'd done her job right?

Jamie turned her mind from useless speculation.

"Mind telling me where we're going?"

She hesitated at his question, but what was the point? "We're going to try and stop another murder."

"Laudable goal. How many of us did you kidnap tonight?"

She sent him a glare.

"Okay then, who else is going to be murdered?"

"The people who set up your kidnapping."

"You want to share a little here?"

"No."

"Right. How are we going to prevent them from being murdered?"

Jamie inhaled. "I have no idea."

Only the barest hint of light streaked the horizon. The fatigue tugging at her brain told Jamie daybreak was fast approaching. The suburban streets were still empty as she steered the car into Tony's subdivision.

Harrison Trent had fallen silent after their last exchange, for which Jamie was grateful. He didn't need to know how rattled she was. None of her extensive training had left her prepared for the reality of almost dying on the job. The stench of the smoke clung to her hair and clothing despite the windows she'd opened to air them out. The knowledge that Kirsten and

Elaine had died because she hadn't done her job well enough was a weight on her soul.

So far, she'd managed to keep the shakes at bay. Unfortunately, she knew she was heading for a meltdown. The only thing that kept her going was the certainty that it wasn't Tony who had set them up to die. Tony and Carolyn were in deadly danger from whoever had.

Turning the corner onto their street sent a new surge of apprehension pouring through her. Their house was near the middle of the block, and it glowed like a Christmas tree. Lights blazed behind the curtained windows on the first floor. Tony and Carolyn were early risers, but not this early.

Harrison Trent straightened in his seat. "It's the house with the lights on, isn't it?"

"Yes."

"Looks like we're expected."

Jamie cruised past slowly while her heart hammered in her chest. Carolyn's dark SUV sat in the driveway. Tony's fancy sports car was probably inside the detached garage along with his souped-up sedan.

"The SUV belongs there?" he asked.

"Yes."

"Then what's wrong?"

"I'm not sure."

She circled the block looking for anything out of place. Every parked car was suspect. She watched for the slightest motion. Nothing. Not even a stray cat or dog disturbed the stillness.

She stared at the house as she drove past again at a crawl. "It's too quiet."

"It's early Saturday morning. What do you expect? Most people sleep in on weekends."

Jamie pulled over at the end of the street. She turned off the headlights, but left the engine running. "Wait here while I check this out."

"Not going to happen."

Her body hummed with tension. "Then take the car. You can leave." After all, there was nothing she could do to stop him.

"As tempting as that offer is, I believe I'll stay with you for now."

"Mr. Trent, I'm serious."

"So am I. I deserve some answers."

She exhaled loudly. "I don't have time for this."

"Then turn off the engine and stop arguing."

Her hand shook as she obeyed. "The people who blew up the farmhouse may be inside there."

"I got that, but you're going in, aren't you?"

"Yes."

"Then I'm going with you. I have a few things to say to these people."

Jamie growled. "You aren't going to be reasonable about this, are you?" She pulled the gun from her ankle strap. He eyed it and her, but didn't appear intimidated.

"I'm a businessman, Jamie. I'm always reasonable. Let's go." He opened the car door.

Jamie saw no option. She couldn't force him to wait, and panic hovered, a mere breath away.

Something was badly wrong inside, she sensed it.

"Let me lead," she ordered. "If anything goes wrong—"

"I'll be right behind you."

She shook her head.

"You wouldn't have another gun, would you?"

"No." The last thing she wanted was a person she couldn't predict at her back armed with a weapon.

Without another word she began running toward the house. Hopefully, anyone seeing them would take them for a pair of early morning joggers trying to beat the August heat and not notice the gun she tried to conceal in her hand.

Passing Tony's house, she saw no sign of movement inside. She went up the driveway of the silent house next door. Trent got points for not asking more questions as Jamie led him around to the back and cut through to Tony and Carolyn's yard. Their kitchen light tossed shadows across the porch and down onto the manicured lawn. Nothing moved inside or out. Fear pulsed with every beat of her heart.

Skipping the back door, she went around to the side entrance where it was dark. Trent remained silent as she pulled out her keys and inserted one in the lock. Jamie stiffened. The door swung open at the first touch without the turn of the key.

Her heart threatened to explode as she eased inside. Muted voices came from the living room. Jamie paused to listen.

The television, she realized when background music started to play. Tony wouldn't be watching television at this hour. Something was horribly wrong.

Staying against the wall, she moved up the stairs to the softly glowing kitchen.

Chapter Three

Harrison gave her space and followed quietly. Jamie was obviously spooked at finding the door unlocked. He was more than a little spooked himself. What was he doing here? He should have taken the car and gone for the police.

Maybe it was the drugs still in his system, or maybe he was punchy from exhaustion, but the night had taken on a surrealism that made thinking straight difficult. This was quite possibly the dumbest thing he'd ever done in his life.

The smell hit him even before Jamie stilled so abruptly that he bumped into her back. Beyond her shoulder he took in the scene with a detached sense of horror.

A crumpled form lay on the tiled floor surrounded by a pool of dark blood. The microwave door gaped open above the body. An unpopped bag of popcorn was still clutched in lifeless fingers.

Harrison forced himself to study the scene and his brain went numb with shock. *Ceecee.* Impossible. That couldn't be Ceecee. Not here. Not lying dead like this.

Ceecee was vibrantly alive. She'd always been an attractive woman, and yes, she'd be in her late fifties now. And her hair had always been dark and soft, her body trim, but always in motion. The summery yellow slacks and casual shirt were so typical of what he remembered, but this couldn't be her.

Ceecee had an infectious laugh. She had a way of listening to someone as if they were the most important person in her world. She'd been his mother's best friend since before he'd been born.

When he was a boy, Ceecee Carillo would

call or turn up every so often no matter where they lived. Their home was always brighter for her visits. His mother was laughing constantly during her stays even when they only sat around the kitchen table, chatting and giggling like a pair of schoolgirls. And Ceecee had always had a present for him when she came. She treated him as if he were another adult, not some boring little kid.

Until the year he turned fourteen. After his kidnapping, she didn't come anymore. He'd thought it was because they'd moved and his mother was afraid to have visitors. He knew she still talked to Ceecee on the phone after that, but she didn't laugh and she always seemed sad afterward.

He'd never asked why Ceecee didn't come anymore. Now, staring at her lifeless body, Harrison realized it was one question he should have asked.

The kitchen was neat and clean. There were no signs of a struggle. It appeared as if someone had walked up behind her as she went to place the popcorn in the microwave and had shot her through the back of the head. Either she knew her killer and didn't fear him, or she never heard him coming.

Harrison glanced at Jamie. She stared at the body through a film of moisture. He had known the dead woman as Ceecee, but Jamie had called her Carolyn. Carolyn Carillo. Ceecee. It must have been his mother's nickname for her.

The gaze Jamie turned to him held a dark well of pain that trapped his tumbling questions in his throat. Ceecee had been important to her as well.

Oh, God, surely not her mother.

Before he could utter a word, Jamie's gaze hardened. She held up a palm, indicating he should wait. The smell of death made his stomach roil. Ceecee was stiff and utterly lifeless. She had been dead for some time.

Apparently, Jamie agreed. She made no move to cross the room. Instead, she glided cautiously toward the entrance beyond the kitchen.

Harrison turned from the scene more slowly, still reeling from the shock of recognition. He watched where he walked as he followed in Jamie's wake. The last thing he wanted to do was step on anything in a crime scene. His stretched nerves screamed at him. They should call the police and leave the scene, but he wasn't going without Jamie. He wanted answers.

Harrison found her in the living room beside a plush leather recliner and the slumped body of an older man. Even from a distance Harrison could see that the man had been killed like Ceecee. The killer had walked up behind his chair and shot him through the temple, no doubt using a silencer.

Jamie lightly touched the man's cheek with a fingertip. Once again, the eyes she turned toward Harrison brimmed with unshed tears. Who were these people to her?

Had Ceecee been married? How could he not even know that much about his mother's oldest friend?

Once more he started to speak. Once more Jamie shook her head sharply and motioned him to stay put.

She flowed up the staircase on silent feet. His stomach twisted at the thought that there might be more bodies up there. He didn't want to follow her up those stairs. He didn't want to see her find more death.

He scanned the cozy living room. Two glasses partially filled with dark liquid sat on the table between the two chairs. If the glasses had once held ice, it had long since melted. The chairs were side by side facing the television set, where an old movie was playing on one of the cable stations. The dialogue and spurts of music were the only sounds in the silent house.

The couple had obviously settled down for the evening to watch television together. At some point Ceecee had gotten up to make popcorn. The killer had probably entered through the side door they had used and shot one after the other.

His gaze fell on the table behind the couch,

where several framed photographs held prominence. The couple appeared much younger in most shots, and so obviously in love. The two wedding photos had been taken sometime in the early sixties. His stomach clenched when his mother's face stared out at him from the group shot. Vibrantly lovely in her youth, she posed beside the bride, obviously Ceecee's maid of honor.

How? Why? All sorts of wild conjectures swirled through his head.

There were several photographs of Jamie as a teenager with her hair long and thick and curling past her shoulders as she posed with the couple. Another showed her in a military dress uniform, looking crisp and solemn. The final photo appeared to be more recent. She stood between the couple in front of a Christmas tree with her hair short and choppy, the way she wore it now. There were no shots of her as a child.

Were these her parents? Some other relatives?

He saw no physical resemblance between them, but they appeared to be a family unit.

Abruptly, he realized Jamie had stopped being silent. She was moving about rapidly overhead as if speed was of the essence. He mounted the stairs quietly.

"Don't touch anything," she ordered, leaving a room at the end of the hall with a duffel bag in her hand.

Her voice sounded unnaturally loud in the stillness of the house, despite the muted irritant of the television in the background.

"I wasn't planning to."

He followed her into what appeared to be the master bedroom. Inside the closet she opened a gun case with a key and pulled out several weapons and ammunition.

"Here." She handed him a 9 mm. "Do you know how to use this?"

His eyes narrowed. "Point this end and pull here. Most five-year-olds have the gist."

"You've never fired a gun."

She said it flatly as if it was a stupid omission. "Shooting a gun never made my to-do list."

"Maybe you'd better give it back."

"I don't think so. Is there a safety on this thing?"

She muttered something under her breath and indicated the switch. "Move this. The gun is fully loaded, so leave it on for now. I don't want you shooting me by mistake."

"Wouldn't think of it."

He jammed the heavy metal object into his waistband, the way he'd seen it done in the movies. Hopefully the gun couldn't go off on its own and blow away something vital.

Scowling, she shoved another weapon in her duffel bag. "If they know we escaped, they'll come back here. They'll know this is where I'd head."

"Who will know?"

"That's what I plan to find out." Her voice was brittle, underscored by anguish. She suddenly whirled on him, her features a mask of pain. "Who *are* you? What makes you worth all these lives?"

Stunned, Harrison gaped at her. "You're blaming me for this?"

"You're the focal point."

He struggled to bank his answering swell of anger as she shoved another gun in the back waistband of her pants beneath her shirt. Boxes of shells went into the duffel bag.

"Let me remind you that *you* kidnapped *me*."

Leaving the bag open, she ignored that and sized him up with eyes that were haunted by grief. "Thirty-six-inch waist?"

He narrowed his eyes. "Thirty-four."

"Close enough." She reached in and pulled out a pair of men's jeans and added them to the bag that already held clothing.

"What are you doing?"

"What does it look like?" She tossed in a couple of shirts as well.

"I have my own clothes."

"Not with you."

He shook his head as she added more items with no wasted motions. "I'm six-one."

"So?"

"The man downstairs—"

The look of pain on her face rocked him back. "His name was Tony. He was five-eleven."

Tony, not Dad. "Who—?"

"Later. We need to move. I don't think they rigged this house to explode or it probably would have by now, but I don't have time to be sure."

Cold swept him.

"Let's go." She closed the duffel bag and handed it to him. "You carry it. I'll take point." She reached the doorway in two strides.

"Why aren't we calling the police?" Why hadn't *he* done that instead of standing around like a brain-dead fool?

She didn't bother responding. His gut coiled as he realized she really did think the house might explode. They exited the way they'd entered with no last glance at either body. If it hadn't been for her obvious grief, he'd have thought she didn't care.

His own mind was numb with what he dimly

recognized as shock. He couldn't help the accompanying fear that this house might blow up at their backs as well.

Instead of running back to her car, Jamie ran to the two-car garage behind the house. She bypassed the zippy bright red sports car and unlocked the large black sedan beside it. "Get in."

"What about your car?"

"It's a rental. We need to get rid of it. Toss the bag in the back."

Harrison obeyed. He climbed in as she opened the garage door with a remote clipped to the visor. "What about the SUV in the driveway behind us?"

"I'll go around it."

He looked back through the darkly tinted windows and swallowed a protest. He'd have sworn there wasn't enough room between the house and the big SUV for this large sedan, but he'd have been wrong. She drove with an impressive precision, scraping neither the house nor the car and barely slowing down in the process.

She braked as soon as she reached her rental car. "Here." She handed him the keys.

"What's to stop me from leaving?"

"Not a thing. I almost wish you would. But you won't survive another twenty-four hours on your own. You seem to be a slow learner, Mr. Trent. Someone wants you dead and they don't care who else they have to kill to make it so."

There was cold certainty in her voice. Harrison didn't understand what was happening here, but he could tell she believed every word she was saying. "Pretty sure of your abilities, aren't you?"

Her expression didn't change. "There's a good chance neither one of us is going to survive the next twenty-four hours, but I have the expertise to try. What about you?"

There was nothing he could say to that.

"There's a gas station not far from here where we can leave the rental."

"You know who's behind these attacks."

She didn't flinch at the accusation. "No."

"You've got some idea." He could see that she did.

"Either follow me or go, but get out of the car."

It was her inner anguish that decided him. "I'll stick with you." He wanted answers and she was going to give them to him one way or another.

Harrison stepped from the sedan and moved to the smaller car. He stayed right behind her as she drove the speed limit out of the development. Obviously, she didn't want to draw any attention to them.

His mind mulled over the little he knew, trying to fit pieces together. There were too many pieces missing, too many answers he might never know. He wished his mother was still alive so he could ask her all the questions filling him.

Pulling into a closed gas station, Jamie motioned him to park along the side where similar cars were stacked two deep. He did and got out of the rental. She left the sedan's engine running, got out, took the rental's keys from him along with the paperwork that sat inside the glove compartment. Dropping everything in a slot in the door of the gas station, she ran back to the sedan. Only then did he see the discreet sign that the station acted as a rental place as well.

"Let's go," she called to him.

He joined her in the sedan. "Where?"

Jamie's response was to pull the car out into the early morning traffic. Harrison saw her fatigue now that the adrenaline rush had begun to fade. "How long have you been up?"

She darted a surprised glance his way. "I'm fine."

"I'm not and I got some sleep before you attacked me."

"I didn't attack you."

"Drugged, abducted, taped and secured in a strange location. What would you call it?"

"My job. We can sleep later."

"You're right about the sleep, anyhow. We need to go to Zoe's apartment."

"Not a chance."

"Stop the car."

Her glare was quelling. "You still don't get it!"

"I get it fine." He interrupted the start of her next tirade. "Someone wants me dead. And that same someone may want *her* dead as well. It's the next place they'll target. We both know that. I'm going there with you or alone. They already believe they killed us," he added over the objection she started to make. "And if they don't, it doesn't matter. I *am* going to Zoe's."

"I'm trying to keep you alive here."

"Try keeping us all alive. Zoe's pregnant."

He didn't know what had made him add that last, but she stilled.

"We're getting married this morning," he reminded her.

"No. You aren't. And before you jump all over me again, your wedding is scheduled for eleven. I was supposed to keep you safe until noon. That should tell you something, Mr. Trent.

Someone does not intend for your wedding to take place."

Harrison forced his fingers to uncurl. "Why not?"

"I don't know! Maybe Tony knew, but Tony's dead." Pain laced her words.

"Who was Tony to you?"

Jamie released a slow breath. "The closest thing I had to a father."

Her voice broke. Automatically, his hand started toward her to offer comfort. He lowered it without touching her. "I'm sorry."

"And I'm sorry about Zoe."

"Zoe isn't dead." She could not be dead.

"I hope not. And you did say you hired a bodyguard for her. Is he any good?"

"Ramsey Inc. is the top security firm in the area."

"Then she has a chance."

His mind relived the barrage of shots in the parking lot over three months ago. Zoe, Artie and he had just split up after leaving the office for the night. He remembered running, throwing himself over Zoe as she went down, terrified he'd been too late to protect his friend.

"I'm going to her apartment."

Jamie swore softly. "This is stupid."

"I'm still going."

She glanced at his face and sighed heavily. "You're a fool. We're both fools," she muttered, conceding defeat. "Give me directions."

Harrison rubbed a hand across his gritty eyes as she turned the car toward Zoe's. Jamie scowled at the early morning drivers starting to make their way onto the roads.

"How is it you don't know of Ramsey Incorporated?" he asked. "They're the most prestigious security firm around here."

She hesitated, then shrugged as if she'd decided the answer didn't matter. "I live and work in California. I was only in town for a visit when Tony asked me to help out."

"And he didn't tell you why?"

"Only that we were protecting you."

"You must have some idea who's behind all this."

Her hesitation was confirmation. "Tony wouldn't say."

"But you have a suspicion."

"That's all it is."

Harrison waited. She muttered something succinct under her breath and turned to look at him as she stopped for a red light. "What do you know about Victor DiMarko?"

The unexpected name rocked him almost as hard as seeing Ceecee dead on her kitchen floor. He jerked as if physically struck. All the air seemed to leave his lungs at once.

Victor DiMarko. Wealthy businessman. Philanderer. Restaurateur. Crime boss. Husband and father. Coldhearted, vicious son of a bitch.

"I see you know the name." Her features went inscrutable once more as she pulled into the intersection. "Tony and Carolyn worked for him until they retired."

It was as if Jamie had thrown a light switch.

Ceecee had worked for Victor DiMarko. No wonder his mother had had little contact with her after his kidnapping all those years ago. With DiMarko's name, everything changed. "You work for Victor DiMarko?"

"No! The company I work for has nothing to do with him or his kind of people." She drew in a deep breath. "I take it you *do* know him."

Somehow Harrison kept his voice even. "I know who he is. We've never met." He'd gone out of his way to see that never happened.

"I thought…"

"What? That I'm in the same line of work?" His jaw muscles worked as anger flashed in his eyes.

"Are you? Glare all you want. Tony said he was helping a friend by arranging your kidnapping. I know he kept in touch with DiMarko. The logical conclusion is that Tony got involved because his former boss asked him for a favor. But maybe I guessed wrong. If you and DiMarko have never met… Were you competing for something? Property? A—"

"No. Nothing." But Harrison's mind continued to whirl with possibilities.

"What about your...Zoe?"

Mentally, Harrison swore. He'd just come to that same possibility. "If there's a connection, it has to be through Wayne Drake."

"How did Zoe know him?"

"She met Drake at a party at my place. He crashed the party, but neither of us knew that at the time because he came in with a group of expected guests and everyone thought he was with someone else. After he was killed and the police told us his background, they theorized he came there to steal something that night and instead latched on to Zoe as a means of getting close to more targets, including me."

"Drake worked for DiMarko?"

"I've no idea." And the thought had never occurred to him until now.

"What would DiMarko gain by killing the two of you?"

"Not a thing." He rubbed at his jaw tiredly. "We're missing something."

"A whole lot of somethings," she agreed. "Where do I turn?"

Harrison indicated the street leading to the apartment building. Jamie drove slowly into the parking lot and tensed. In front of the building, marked and unmarked police cars lined the fire lane.

Heart thumping painfully in his chest, Harrison picked out the window of Zoe's temporary unit. Lights blazed from the windows. Even from this distance he could see people moving around inside. His heart wrenched. "Zoe."

Jamie ignored the whispered plea and kept driving.

"What are you doing? Turn around. Go back!"

"So they can kill you, too?" she snapped. "Not going to happen."

Rage and grief filled him.

"Forget it, tough guy. I just lost the two people I care most about in this world. I'm sorry you may have lost someone, too, but you're an intelligent man. Start thinking with your head. Zoe's either dead or she isn't. Either way, you can't help her right now. All you can do is put yourself in harm's way and make it easy for them to get you, too. How is that going to help anyone? We don't even know who they are or why they're doing this. And I don't think your Zoe is dead. I didn't see a coroner's unit. Think!"

Jamie was relieved when the lash of her words seemed to have an effect. Some of the anger began to fade from his features.

"We need to tell the police what we know."

His voice was calm despite the emotions swirling in the depths of his eyes.

"Which is absolutely nothing."

"Victor DiMarko—"

"Is going to have an alibi cast in granite, I promise you. And for all we know, he may be innocent. The police will question him. What sort of answers do you think DiMarko will have even if he's guilty? We need to stay alive if we're going to figure out who is behind all this."

Harrison fell silent. Jamie snaked another look in his direction and found his eyes were as closed as his fists. She drove aimlessly, trying to think what to do. Fatigue sucked at her mind, mingling with the pit of depression that threatened to drown her completely.

Tony and Carolyn were gone. Her eyes burned with unshed tears. The lump in the back of her throat felt like a boulder. She hadn't felt this alone since she'd left her abusive stepfather behind and begun living on the streets. She wanted to howl with the grief shredding her insides, but this wealthy man's life might very well depend on her and her skills. Protecting him was the last thing Tony had asked of her.

She swallowed hard and sought inner calm the way Carolyn had taught her. She had to clear her mind. If they were up against the forces of a man like DiMarko, then it was probably only a matter of time, but she wanted that time!

Anger shunted her other emotions aside. She was not going down without a fight. She'd learned a long time ago that the only one she could rely on was herself. There were worse things than being alone, but she would miss them so much.

Jamie had no idea how long she'd been driving when a glance at her silent passenger showed he was either asleep or lost in his own grief. And no wonder. He'd said his Zoe was pregnant. If she was dead, he'd lost his child as well as his lover. Her heart ached for him, but she had no comfort to offer.

Ahead was a fast food drive-through. Tired beyond words, she pulled into the line of cars waiting for service.

Trent opened his eyes. "What are you doing?"

"I need coffee. My thoughts are going in circles. What do you want to eat?"

For a long second, he said nothing. "Just coffee. Black."

She nodded. When her turn came, she ordered two breakfast sandwiches and two orange juices as well as the coffees. She took the cardboard tray from the kid behind the window and gave it to Trent while the kid made change from her twenty. Trent said nothing until she'd pulled away from the window and found a place to park near the back of the lot.

"What are you doing now?" he asked.

"Having breakfast." She took a sandwich and handed him the bag.

"I'm not hungry."

"Neither am I, but our bodies and our minds need something besides caffeine to help us function. Especially yours."

He cocked his head.

"You were drugged, Trent. You need to eat that sandwich."

He regarded her silently. Jamie unwrapped hers and took a bite. He watched her chew and swallow without moving. She reached for the small cup of orange juice, peeled back the foil and took a long swallow, draining the juice.

"I should leave."

She held his gaze, pleased that her hand set the empty cup down without shaking. "We've already had this discussion. I can't stop you."

The silence stretched. After what felt like forever, his hand reached into the bag and pulled out the second sandwich. Jamie breathed a silent sigh of relief.

They ate in silence. Afterward, he gathered the refuse and carried it to a nearby trash can. She waited to start the engine until he slid back inside.

"We need to decide what to do," she told him.

"Take me to the church. If Zoe is still alive, she'll go there."

"So will the police and the people who tried to kill you."

"Not if they think I'm dead."

"And if they don't?"

His jaw set with determination. "Artie and Carter will be there. People we can trust."

"Are you sure of that?"

His eyes narrowed.

"You can't afford to trust anyone until we figure out what's going on."

"I can trust them."

She shot him a tight look and hesitated, weighing their options. His Zoe might have some answers if they could find her without getting killed. But would she really go to the church? The police certainly would and they'd have questions, a lot of them. By now they certainly knew Harrison had been abducted.

She couldn't see another way around the only answer that presented itself. "I need to call Victor DiMarko."

She thought he tensed, but she couldn't be sure. He stared at her without saying a word.

"If DiMarko had nothing to do with what's happened, he'll make a formidable ally. He always treated Tony and Carolyn with respect."

"And if he had them killed and me kidnapped?"
Jamie hesitated.

"The man is a crime boss, Jamie."

"If he wanted you dead, you'd be dead. He could have given me something that would have killed you the minute I injected it into your bloodstream. Or, as the bartender, I could have slipped you a lethal drug with your first drink. There's more going on here than a simple murder. Why involve Tony and Carolyn in the first place? They've been retired for years now. DiMarko has all sorts of people at his beck and call. I don't suppose it's occurred to you that Zoe might be behind your kidnapping."

Harrison's silence filled the car.

"Did you by any chance change your will in her favor?"

Jamie liked that he took his time and considered her words before answering.

"No."

"No, what?"

"The police were at Zoe's place."

"Which is where they would be once you were reported missing."

"All the more reason for me to go to the church."

She swore softly before putting the car in gear. "I knew you were going to say that. If you get us killed I'll haunt you through eternity. Where is this church?"

TRAFFIC WAS HEAVY. The Saturday back-to-school shoppers were out in force so Jamie had to pay attention. The silence that stretched between her and the man at her side was surprisingly comfortable. Harrison Trent wasn't a stupid person. If he felt he had to go to the church, she'd take him there. Maybe she was wrong about the danger. She really hoped she was wrong about the danger.

As they approached the large stone building that jutted out on an island surrounded by traffic, she glanced at her passenger. "I'm going to circle the block."

"All right."

Tension sang along her nerves. Her eyes

panned the area, alert to every movement. A pedestrian suddenly darted across the road. Traffic braked sharply, coming to an abrupt standstill in both directions. Jamie's gaze swept the tall building alongside them. Even with that, she nearly missed the glint of sun on metal.

"There! Look!" She aimed a finger at the roof of the building across the street from the front of the church.

Harrison leaned forward, peering through the windshield. "I see it."

The sniper was nearly invisible, so she was relieved Trent saw him as well. She put the car in motion once more as traffic began to move. Already committed, she circled the block. A car with darkly tinted windows sat across from the side entrance to the church. Jamie pointed out the figure inside. He was nothing more than an outline, but there was no doubt in her mind that a second gunman waited behind the dark glass.

"Somebody knows we made it out of the farmhouse."

Chapter Four

"Stop the car!"

Jamie's head whipped in Harrison's direction. His hand was already on the door handle.

"Zoe's walking into an ambush!"

"Listen to me! *If* she's still alive. *If* she's not in police custody. And *if* she's stupid enough to show up here after something obviously happened at her place. Think it through, Trent! You can't save her if you're dead."

Her fierce words stayed his hand.

"I'll park the car. We'll find the nearest phone and call the police. We do it my way and your Zoe will be safe and so will we."

He released his hold on the handle with reluctance as Jamie turned onto a side street and pulled up before a fire hydrant. "You'll get towed."

"That's the least of our worries. Let's go."

Together they ran back toward a busy pharmacy on the corner. Jamie ignored the line of people waiting to check out and approached the cashier. "We need to use your telephone. It's an emergency."

"We don't have a pay phone," the bored teen behind the counter told her without looking up.

"I need the police. Now!"

The kid gaped at her tone and the woman next in line jerked to attention. "I have a cell phone you can use." She quickly rummaged through her oversized purse. "Here."

"Thank you." Taking the cell phone, she pressed 911 and told the dispatcher about the sniper on the roof and the car on the side street. There wasn't another sound in the store as every head focused on her. Giving the dispatcher a phony name, she closed the cell phone and returned it to the bemused woman.

"Thank you. Let's go," she urged Harrison.

Excited voices filled the unnatural silence in their wake as Harrison followed her out the door. Before they could reach the car, a police cruiser with lights flashing raced past, heading toward the intersection.

"We need to get out of here in case they cordon off the area."

"I should have called Zoe's cell phone to warn her."

"We'll find another phone."

Once back in the car, Harrison closed his eyes, pinching the bridge of his nose as if he had a headache. His body was tight with tension. The events of the past few hours were taking their toll. The drug, lack of sleep and concern for his fiancée gave his features a haggard, gray cast. She suspected he was starting to crash. Her own eyes felt gritty from lack of sleep, and she was working on her own headache as they drove off.

"Where are we going?" he asked.

"I'm not sure. We reek of smoke. It's the first

thing a police officer will notice if we're stopped. There's probably a pickup order out for both of us, so we can't risk being stopped. My license to carry concealed is for California."

"I don't have one at all."

"The last thing we want is to explain to the local defenders of law and order why we are armed to the teeth. You're tired and so am I."

For once, Harrison Trent nodded instead of arguing.

"I think we should find a motel room, call Zoe and shower off this smoke stench. We'll decide where to go from there."

"I don't like it."

"What's the alternative?"

He sighed and closed his eyes again. "I can't think of one."

Relieved, Jamie drove until she found a two-story motel outside Chantilly that boasted small suites rather than just rooms. Each unit had its own entrance.

Eyes still closed, Trent agreed to wait in the

car while she registered them. "Don't fall asleep. I can't carry you."

He opened one eye. "Were you a drill sergeant in the military by any chance?"

Surprised, she tipped her head to one side. Then she remembered her service photo on Carolyn's picture table. "Military police."

"Of course." He closed his eyes.

When she returned a few minutes later, he was still awake and even insisted on carrying the bag inside the room for her. Their suite had two rooms that could be separated by sliding panel doors. The sitting area consisted of a small couch, two chairs, lamps and scattered tables. A small dining area was at the far end with a miniature kitchenette to one side. The television had been built into the counter that separated the kitchen from the main sitting area. In the second room was a king-size bed and bathroom.

"I'll take the first shower while you make your call."

With a nod at Jamie, Harrison sank down in the chair beside the telephone and started to dial Zoe's number. He stopped before he completed the sequence. Instead he dialed Artie's cell phone number.

"Harrison? Where are you? Are you okay?"

The deep concern in his friend's voice was warming. "Tired, but unharmed. Are you at the church?"

"No. When you disappeared, Zoe called off the wedding. We thought you'd been kidnapped. What happened?"

"I was kidnapped."

There was a beat of silence. "The police are still here. I'll get—"

"Not right now. Is Zoe all right?"

"Yes, other than worried about you."

"So she didn't go to the church."

"I don't think so. You want to explain what's going on?"

Harrison debated. Artie probably knew as much about him as anyone, but even Artie didn't know of his relationship to DiMarko. He preferred to keep it that way. "Not at the moment."

Artie's voice hardened. "They had to take my entire staff to the hospital last night. I think I deserve some answers."

"Were they hurt?"

"They were drugged, but they're all recovering. None of them remember a thing."

Harrison relaxed, but frowned. "You weren't drugged?"

"I wasn't here. My sister, Sybil, showed up shortly after you went upstairs last night. I had to go with her to bail my nephew out of jail. Tad and his friends got in some trouble and Sybil's husband is out of town. The police figure the intruders came for you right after we left. It looked like a professional job. So, how did you get away?"

Harrison ran a hand through his hair. "It's a long story, Artie. I'm in the middle of something here and I don't have time to go into it right now. Does anyone know you're talking to me?"

"No. I was just getting ready to hop in the shower."

"Good. Don't say anything about this call."

Artie's voice sharpened. "Why not?"

"Have you talked to Carter?"

"He's here. I called him to help me get Tad out of jail. I took Sybil's car and dropped them off at their place last night only to come home to cops and ambulances. Carter hadn't even made it back to bed when I called him. He's been here all night."

"Let me give him a quick call."

"And Zoe?"

"Especially Zoe. I'm not sure what's going on, Artie. The important thing is to keep her safe."

"Is your kidnapping related to what happened to Drake?"

"I don't know yet."

"Zoe's with the bodyguard Ramsey sent out. You want me to call them?"

"No, I'll do it."

"Then how can I help?"

"Until I know more, there isn't anything anyone can do at the moment. Let me call you back." He disconnected to find Jamie watching him from the opening between the rooms, holding what appeared to be a man's shaving kit. There were shadows beneath her eyes, lines of fatigue marring her smooth skin, and her crazy hair was sticking up at odd angles, yet he couldn't help thinking she was still the most fascinating woman he'd ever met.

"Zoe's okay?"

Harrison nodded. "The police are at Artie's. They know I was kidnapped."

"Naturally. Who's Carter?"

"My lawyer."

"Okay then. If everything's all right, I'll take a quick shower. You could make us some coffee."

Distracted, he nodded and punched in Carter's cell phone number. The moment his friend answered, he spoke quickly.

"It's Harrison. Don't let anyone know you're talking to me."

There was a beat of silence. "Excuse me," Carter's calm voice told someone. "I need to take this call."

Harrison waited, listening to the background voices but unable to catch any words. He'd seen enough movies to imagine the scene with police standing around waiting for a ransom call. A door closed, shutting the noises out, and Carter's voice filled his ears. "Are you okay?"

"Tired, but fine." He rubbed his temple, trying to ignore the pounding in his head.

"What happened?"

"Long story. I don't have time to explain at the moment."

"Are you free to talk?"

He realized what Carter was asking. "Yes. We got away."

"We?"

"It's complicated. I may need you to finesse a few things from a legal standpoint."

The silence was telling.

"Carter, set up whatever protection Zoe needs—money, additional protection, anything."

"Talk to me, Harrison."

"I've acquired a bodyguard and we're working on the situation. Is there any way you can keep this under wraps and call off the police? Tell them… I don't know. Make something up." He rubbed the bristles on his jaw tiredly. "Tell them I'm free and I'll be in to explain as soon as I can."

"That's not going to fly, Harrison."

"Then lie. I don't care what you tell them, but I have to take care of something before I talk to the police. The kidnapping isn't what it looks like."

Carter's voice went low and quiet. Harrison knew him well. Carter was coldly furious. "What it looks like is someone drugged five people and put four of them in the hospital with no memory of what happened. They kidnapped a sixth person who just happens to be a very wealthy friend of mine, and attacked his fiancée."

Harrison jerked. "Zoe was attacked?"

"A pair of armed men showed up at the apartment. She and her bodyguard got away, but that's pretty much all I know because *she* doesn't want to talk to the police, either. She called Artie around eight o'clock this morning, learned you were missing and asked him to call off the wedding. Now talk to me."

"It's a family matter."

"*Whose* family? You don't *have* any family. Do you?" he added after a beat.

"None I want to claim. I'll call you back when I know something definite."

"Don't hang up. Harrison?"

He hung up and stared at the wall. Someone had gone after Zoe as well as him. But why? None of it made any sense.

Who are you that you're worth all these lives?

Jamie's earlier anguished words echoed in his head. His fingers curled in frustration.

If DiMarko wanted him dead, he could have arranged it anytime over the past several years. The only thing that was different right now was that Harrison hadn't been engaged to marry Zoe until a few weeks ago. Yet the threats to her had come shortly after she started dating Wayne Drake.

Drake had to be the common denominator, but Drake was dead. Harrison was missing something here. If only he wasn't so tired.

He looked toward the bedroom. The shower was still running in the bathroom. It was tempting to get up and walk out the door. Jamie didn't deserve to be caught up in his problems. Ceecee and her husband were dead because someone was cleaning up as they went along. They'd tried to kill Jamie as well. She was a loose end they couldn't afford to ignore.

What if Ceecee had been behind his kidnapping for some reason? Could she have been trying to protect him? But that pointed the finger right back at DiMarko, and his father had known for years where he was.

Harrison shut his eyes. He needed to tell Jamie about his connection to Ceecee. Maybe it would give her a different slant on whatever

Tony had told her. He should have told Jamie about his relationship with her foster mother right away, but things had happened fast and… And he hadn't trusted her before. Did he trust her now? Could he trust his memory of Ceecee?

He hadn't known Ceecee at all as an adult, but he'd adored her as a kid. She'd brought a special joy into his mother's life as well as his own. Her senseless death was an affront to that memory. If Ceecee was dead because of him, Harrison owed it to both their memories to see that someone paid for stilling her infectious laughter forever.

Anger was a good barrier against the fatigue muddling his thoughts. A shower might help. A few hours of sleep would help more, but there wasn't time. Someone had gone after Zoe.

She was one of the few people in the world he did trust completely. He'd thought he was protecting her and her unborn child by offering to marry her and give the baby a name. Now he could see it would have been a mistake, and not just because he was so drawn to Jamie.

And he was. He had been the moment he'd set eyes on her. No one had ever captivated him that way. Not that he would act on that attraction while he was engaged to Zoe. He shook his head at his wandering thoughts. He needed to focus.

The wedding appeared to be the catalyst for his kidnapping no matter who was responsible. Who stood to gain if the wedding didn't take place?

Opening his eyes, he dialed Zoe's cell phone number. Relief flooded him when she answered.

"Zoe? It's Harrison. Are you all right?"

"I'm fine. Where are you? Are *you* okay? I saw you at the church."

"You went there?"

"Of course. I knew you'd go there if you could. What happened at Artie's house? How did you get away?"

"It's a long story. Let me talk to Wickliff." It would be quicker to explain to her bodyguard what he wanted her to do. Zoe could teach stubborn to a mule.

"Wickliff's in the hospital. Wayne's people showed up at the condo last night. We had to run and—"

"Where are you?" he interrupted, jacking up straight in the chair.

"In Arlington."

"Are you alone?"

"No, Xavier's with me. We're—"

"Who's Xavier?" But the heavy tread of footsteps came to a halt outside the door to his unit. The shadowy shape he saw outlined beyond the curtained window was no maid. Adrenaline poured through him.

"I'll call you back," he told Zoe. "Call Carter Hughes. He'll—"

The person outside stuck a key card in the door. Harrison hung up. In two strides he was at the door, flinging it open.

A heavyset man with a suitcase took a hasty step back. "Oops. I'm sorry." He gazed at the door number in consternation. "I got the wrong room. I wanted 115, not 113."

Harrison stared, seeing only honest dismay as the man squinted at the numbers.

"I'm really sorry to have disturbed you. My mistake."

The stranger was holding a travel case. He moved to the next door down, pushed the card in the lock and hastily disappeared inside. Harrison stood there for several seconds while his breathing steadied. Only then did he step back and close his door.

Reaction left him shaken. He'd been ready to rip the stranger's head off with his bare hands. Thankfully, he hadn't thought to pull out the gun Jamie had given him. That would have really torn it.

He took a deep breath and released it slowly. If *he'd* reacted with such primitive rage, it was a good thing it had been him and not Jamie who'd gone to the door. G.I. Jamie would have pulled a gun for sure and the police would have been all over them.

Jamie was like no one he'd ever met. Tough as steel, yet inherently feminine.

Looking at the phone, he decided to wait until his heart stopped racing to call Zoe back. He set the coffeepot brewing and prowled the room, unable to sit still. Entering the bedroom, he found Jamie's bag open on the bed. Her clean clothes were neatly stacked on the edge of the dresser. He paused at the sight of the very feminine lacy bra on top of a matching set of silk panties.

"Not exactly military issue." The frilly wisps of material looked incongruous sitting beside a pair of guns and a knife in a sheath.

Jamie intrigued him. She was decisive, methodical and possibly lethal, yet full of fascinating contradictions. He'd been drawn to something about her from the first time he'd laid eyes on her.

And that was not a good direction for his thoughts to be taking while he was engaged to Zoe. He stilled, shocked by the realization his subconscious had probed. Used to making logical decisions and working them out, he hadn't let himself fully contemplate the negative ramifications of marrying Zoe.

She was his friend. Her baby needed a father. Neither of them had ever formed a permanent alliance and they worked well together. The solution had seemed obvious.

Had he made a bad decision for both of them? Carnal temptations didn't worry him. He'd never cheat on his wife and he knew Zoe held similar beliefs, but were they cheating themselves by settling for an arrangement rather than something deeper? Until this moment, he'd have said no.

Troubled, Harrison pulled the pair of men's jeans from the bag and frowned at the worn material. They'd be loose in the waist and short in the legs, but they were clean. Jamie had even thought to toss in a bag of toiletries for him. Impressive for someone who'd been worried at the time that the house might blow up around them.

The shower stopped, bringing him out of

thoughts. He gathered Tony's clothes and the man's toiletry kit and waited. Seconds later the bathroom door opened on a waft of steam.

"Oh. I didn't think you'd be off the phone so soon."

Jamie stood wrapped in a plain white towel. She paused in the act of rubbing at her short, spiky hair with a smaller, matching towel. Her sleek skin glowed pink from the hot water, sprinkled with beaded drops that dripped from her hair. Small, firm breasts pushed against the rough terry cloth fabric. His groin tightened.

He'd been right. Last night would have been much more interesting if Jamie had been one of the strippers.

Her eyes narrowed in clear warning. "Forget it, Trent. I just forgot to take my clean clothes in with me."

"Did I say anything?"

She looked pointedly at his pants. "You're engaged, remember?"

"Engaged does not mean dead," he told her

mildly. "Nor does an erection mean I'm going to act on it."

"Good thinking."

She scooped up her clothes and weapons and disappeared back into the bathroom. The image of those long, elegantly shaped legs stayed on his retinas long after the door had closed. He shook his head to clear it of the clean scent of shampoo and coconut, of all things. Instantly, his head began to pound again in earnest. He was more tired than he'd realized. Once he got some sleep, the world would start making sense again.

Leaving his clothes and his gun in a pile where hers had been, he poured himself a cup of black coffee and sipped at the hot brew, hoping the caffeine would jolt his brain back on track. He'd need all his wits if he was going to deal with Victor DiMarko.

He debated calling Zoe back, but he was too unsettled to talk to her at the moment. She was safe. That was all he needed to know. Carter and Artie would see to it she stayed that way.

Jamie exited the bathroom a few minutes later dressed in black slacks and a plain, loose-fitting black T-shirt. Her damp hair stood on end as if she'd been running her fingers through it. "All yours."

"Thanks." He handed her a cup of coffee.

"Mmm. Thank *you*."

He lifted his clothes from the dresser and couldn't resist the desire to rattle her composure just a little. "I liked the towel look better."

"I'm sure you did."

She didn't rattle. His lips lifted. "Do you have a last name, Jamie?"

"Yes." And she crossed into the living area without a backward glance.

He made it all the way to a wry smile as he stepped into the bathroom. Jamie was a fasci-nating enigma, but he was very good with puzzles. And letting his thoughts drift in her direction was easier than thinking about the coming confrontation with Victor DiMarko.

JAMIE WAS ANGRILY PACING the living area when he left the bathroom a short time later in his ill-fitting clothes. He set his dirty laundry on the dresser and tucked the gun in the back of his waistband underneath the shirt he wore outside the loose pants. "What's wrong?"

"The house staff won't put me through to DiMarko."

"Do you think calling him was such a good idea?"

She stopped pacing and raised her head. "Got a better one?"

"We'll go to see him."

"If they won't let me talk to him on the phone, they certainly won't let us in to see him. His place is better fortified than Fort Bragg."

"Maybe so, but they'll let me see him."

Her lips pursed. "Because you're wealthy?"

"No. Because he's my biological father."

Chapter Five

"Victor DiMarko is your father?"

Jamie gaped as if he'd sprouted horns and a tail.

"Biologically speaking," he admitted gruffly. He'd never told anyone that before. "But not in any real sense of the word. I've never met him."

She exhaled softly. "Okay. I don't even know what to say to that."

"There's nothing to say. Unfortunately, it's a fact. But it means he'll see me."

"I wouldn't be so sure."

"He's been trying to see me for years."

"And you've been brushing him off? Brave man."

"I'm glad you can joke about it."

"Who's joking?" But she said it with a curve to her lips.

"Seriously, I've been thinking about this, and while I can see him sending thugs to kidnap me, Jamie, I don't see him blowing up a house around me. There's no reason."

"Thugs?"

Raising his eyebrows, Harrison shrugged. "Okay, attractive thugs, but you did drug me and cart me off against my will."

She muttered something under her breath.

"What was that?"

Jamie cast him a dark look. "Let's go talk to him."

Harrison hesitated. "Jamie, we don't want to do or say anything foolish when we see him. As you said earlier, Victor DiMarko can be a very dangerous man."

"So can the people around him, but while I don't think I've passed my quota for doing foolish things just yet, I'm not totally stupid."

Harrison felt a frisson of concern crawl down his back at her dark expression.

"I can be dangerous, too. We should hang on

to this place for the night. We may need a place no one knows about as an emergency bolt hole."

"I don't like the sound of that."

"Objection noted, but I'm a bodyguard, not a miracle worker. You have no idea what sort of reception we're going to get. Do you?"

He thought of Ceecee dead on her kitchen floor. "No."

"Okay then. I'm thinking we should try the Silver Pelican first. It's DiMarko's flagship restaurant. He keeps his main office there."

Harrison knew.

"I realize you don't owe me any explanations, but how did someone like you come to be related to someone like him?"

"I assume in the usual way."

She scowled at him.

"My mother had a brief affair with him when she was young. She told me she was waiting tables and going to college at the time and he used to come into the place where she was working. When she learned he had children with his wife of several years, she moved away without telling him she was pregnant."

And until today he'd never had a reason to question that story. It could still be true, of course, but if she and Ceecee had been childhood friends it seemed more likely that she'd met DiMarko through Ceecee. Did it make any difference? Nothing could change the fact that his mother had loved him and had given him the best she could provide.

"You're sure Victor DiMarko knows you're his son?"

He nodded grimly. "When I was fourteen I was kidnapped on my way home from school."

She glanced up quickly. "Am I detecting a pattern here?"

Harrison shrugged. "He wasn't behind the kidnapping, but my mother figured he was the reason for it. There was no way she could pay a ransom demand on what she earned, so she called him instead of the police."

"What happened?"

"He refused to help."

Her jaw sagged. She started to say something and stopped.

"Not what you were expecting to hear?"

"Not at all," she agreed. "The DiMarkos are supposed to be all about family, according to Tony."

"Bastard sons aren't included." He shrugged. "It didn't matter since I was able to get away on my own." But he'd never forgotten that his father hadn't cared enough to come to his rescue.

"Someday I'd like to hear that story."

"Maybe someday I'll tell you. The bottom line is that my mother and I left town as soon as I made my way home. We moved around a lot after that."

Jamie said nothing for a long time. Her gaze was troubled. "I never had any direct dealings with the DiMarkos. I've met them a few times and Victor was always nice to me. I know he treated Tony and Carolyn well. They liked him." She winced apologetically.

"They weren't related to him." He kept inflection from his voice, but she cast him a sharp glance nonetheless.

"I can understand why you'd be bitter."

That surprised him. "I'm not bitter. I'm grateful he left me and my mother alone. She didn't like to talk about him, but after I was kidnapped and saw how unhappy she was, I did my own research. I learned enough to figure out he'd built his fortune on the lives of others. I've never wanted any part of it or him. That said, if he's behind what's happened, he owes me and I *will* collect."

Jamie shivered. She wondered if Harrison knew how much he hated his father. She was tempted to turn the car around right then and there and take the first flight back to California. But Carolyn and Tony were dead. Someone had to pay for their murder, and DiMarko just might have the answers they needed.

"You don't have to come with me," he told her gently. "In fact, it might be better if I were to see him on my own."

"No." The memory of their lifeless bodies stiffened her spine. "I have a debt of my own to collect."

"You aren't going to do something reckless, are you?"

"Define reckless."

"Shooting first and asking questions later?"

"I have more control than that, Mr. Trent."

"Harrison."

"Bellman."

He blinked at the non sequitur. "What?"

"My last name is Bellman. If we're wrong about DiMarko and he kills me, I thought you ought to know."

"No one is going to kill you."

She blinked at the fervor in his voice. She wasn't used to being defended by anyone, let alone so forcefully. It rattled her. "I told you, I'm a professional."

"I believe you."

She turned to face him as traffic came to a stop in front of her. Something in his steady gaze caused a flutter low in her stomach.

No! She couldn't afford for this incredibly sexy, terribly wealthy man to be attracted to her. Not only was she way out of his league socially and economically, she wasn't as experienced as he would expect. She was no virgin, but worked hard to be seen as one of the guys, or failing that as the ice maiden she'd been called more than once.

A relationship with Harrison Trent was out of the question. Even without a pregnant fiancée, Harrison was heartbreak waiting to happen to someone like her.

The light changed. Lifting her chin, she drew on her stiff bodyguard persona and accelerated slowly. "Keep it in mind, Harrison. I'll watch your back."

"And I'll watch yours."

Spoken in that sexy tone, it wasn't what she wanted to hear.

THIS LATE IN THE AFTERNOON they had no trouble parking in the large lot behind the Silver Pelican restaurant. In the formal lobby, the hostess's podium stood empty. Harrison nodded toward the right and the bar that was visible around the corner. Two men sat at the far end talking to the attractive woman behind the bar. They had half-finished plates of food in front of them. All three looked up as they approached.

One of the men stood and came forward. "Help you?"

"We're looking for Victor DiMarko," Harrison told him.

He hadn't said it loudly, but everyone seemed to come to instant attention. The quiet one rose and joined his companion, sizing them up with suspicious eyes. "He's not here."

They had *bodyguard* stamped all over them. Harrison didn't glance at Jamie, holding the men's attention. "Where can we find him?"

"Who wants to know?"

"Harrison Trent."

The woman drifted out from behind the bar and disappeared toward the back of the restaurant. Both men tensed. They knew his name. That wasn't reassuring.

"Cade, get Lyle," the talkative one ordered. The other man immediately trotted after the bartender.

"I don't want to see Lyle," Harrison told him calmly. "I want to see Victor."

"I told you, he isn't here."

"Where can I find him?"

"Call and make an appointment."

Harrison bared his teeth. He stepped closer. "I don't have time to mess with appointment secretaries. I need to see DiMarko now."

"Then turn around."

Jamie whirled toward the voice that had come from behind them. Her hand started for a weapon. Harrison gave her full marks for not completing the action. The others had noticed and at least one hand had duplicated her actions. He turned slowly.

While he had never met either of his half brothers, he knew immediately that he was looking at one of them. Similar dark hair, lean build and Harrison's own familiar brown eyes stared back at him.

Those eyes widened in shock.

"You aren't the right DiMarko, either," he told his brother. "Gordon, isn't it?"

He was younger than Lyle by several years and only a few years older than Harrison himself. Gordon's features were so similar to his own that it would be impossible to deny their shared heritage.

Gordon was good. Other than the initial shock, he masked his thoughts perfectly. "What do you want with my father?"

"That's between me and him," Harrison told him evenly.

"My father doesn't keep secrets."

"I'm surprised you can say that with a straight face."

Gordon flushed.

"Tell me how to reach your father."

But it was another new voice that answered, once again from behind him. "I don't think so."

Without turning his head, Harrison knew his oldest half brother, Lyle, was standing there. He didn't know if they'd planned it, or if serendipity had placed Jamie and him between the men, but given the bodyguards who had returned to the room and were closing ranks, the home team had a distinctly uncomfortable advantage.

Harrison forced himself to appear relaxed. Without turning around he replied, "Why don't you let Victor decide?"

"Not going to happen. Take your girlfriend and go," Lyle ordered.

Harrison turned slowly. He kept his movements deliberate. He didn't want anyone getting trigger-happy here. Lyle was shorter and stockier than his brother with an overabundance of muscles that were starting to run to fat. A former weight lifter, Harrison judged. There was no denying the family stamp here, either. Nor the intense dislike that practically sheeted off Lyle. Harrison hadn't expected a warm welcome, but this much animosity came as a surprise. "You know who I am."

"My father's little bastard," Lyle agreed. "Yeah. We know all about you. So what? You aren't welcome here. Get lost."

"So much for brotherly love."

Lyle closed the distance between them. "You are *not* my brother."

"Genetics aside, there's nothing I'd like to agree with more. I still need to see your father."

Confident that Jamie had his back, Harrison kept his attention on Lyle. This was the brother to watch.

"That's not going to happen."

"I have business with Victor."

"What business?"

Harrison didn't respond.

Lyle puffed out his chest. "I run things when he isn't around. He's not, so you'll have to deal with me."

"I'm the one who needs to see him," Jamie interjected before Harrison could respond.

Lyle's eyes narrowed. He looked past Harrison to glare at Jamie. "Yeah? Who are you? Another of his cheap sluts?"

The words found their target as he'd intended. Harrison wanted to plant his fist in those pudgy features. Only the knowledge that Lyle was hoping he'd do exactly that held his temper.

"Didn't the bastard here tell you how we deal with by-blows?" Lyle continued. He shoved Harrison with the heel of his hand as he spoke. Harrison knocked the hand away. He had to block the roundhouse swing that followed.

He hadn't expected a donnybrook, but a part of him welcomed the opportunity for a physical release for some of his pent-up tension. However, even as he followed the block with a short jab to the other man's solar plexus, he knew they were in trouble. He could take Lyle, but once the others jumped into the fray it would be all over.

A low, feminine voice froze everyone in place before Lyle could recover.

"What's going on here? Lyle, what do you

think you're doing? This is a restaurant, not the gym! Stop this instant! You know better. Anyone could walk in."

Lyle froze, fist pulled back at his side. Harrison stepped back to put the bar behind him so he could keep his gaze on Lyle as well as the others. There was hatred in his half brother's eyes.

"Take him out back," Lyle ordered his companions.

"Mrs. DiMarko." Jamie spoke quickly. "I'm Jamie Bellman, Carolyn and Tony's…" She hesitated as if unsure what relationship to claim.

"Their foster daughter, yes."

"We didn't come here to cause trouble. Harrison and I need to speak with your husband as soon as possible. It's important."

"Harrison?"

The fight drained from Lyle and was replaced by another sort of tension altogether. Harrison risked a look toward the woman who was his father's wife. "Harrison Trent, Mrs. DiMarko," he told her.

Harrison had seen her picture in the paper once, but the photograph hadn't done her justice. Iris DiMarko either had extraordinary genes or an excellent plastic surgeon. Possibly both. For a woman in her sixties, she could pass for late thirties. Her sleek brown hair was swept up on top of her head in a simple, flattering style that left wispy bangs gracing her forehead. An elegant, expensive-looking ivory sheath flattered a trim figure she carried with poise and grace. A bit taller and she could have been a superstar runway model.

It took him a moment to realize she wasn't alone. The force of her personality all but eclipsed the younger, attractive woman at her side. Someone who could only be another bodyguard stood behind her. Harrison's gaze returned to the younger woman, who must be his half sister, Fay DiMarko. She could have been her mother's sister instead of his.

Fay was the middle child and the only girl. Fortunately, the family genetics were softened considerably on her strong features. She tossed long, slinky black hair back over her shoulder and stared at him with a blank expression. Her mother might dominate the room, but when they finally got around to looking, most men would find Fay every bit as attractive.

"It's so nice to finally meet you, Mr. Trent." Iris DiMarko stepped forward and extended a warm, soft hand. Only because he was watching her closely did he detect tension behind the firm, impersonal handshake. "My husband has looked forward to this opportunity for some time."

"Too bad the rest of the clan doesn't feel the same way," Jamie muttered.

Iris pretended she hadn't heard the comment and Harrison managed to control the urge to smile. "Call me Harrison," he invited.

"And you must call me Iris."

The irony didn't escape him. The only person in his family who had a true reason to dislike him was being the most gracious, even if she wasn't being entirely sincere.

"Please, won't you both have a seat? Cade, be a dear and bring us some coffee, please. Arturo, you may go to the kitchen with him. I'll be fine. Mr. Trent and Ms. Bellman are my guests."

Her bodyguard gave Harrison and Jamie a hard look before complying with his dismissal.

"Lyle, I believe you and Gordon have some things to take care of in the office? There's a rather nasty storm approaching. Lorne, are the umbrellas down on the deck? Would you check please?"

In seconds she had cleared the room of everyone but Lyle and the four of them. For the first time, Harrison realized how dark the room had grown. He'd been too busy to notice before, but a gust of wind forcefully rattled the windows, highlighting the troubled black sky beyond.

"You're going to sit down with him?" Lyle demanded in outrage.

There was bite to her tone as she turned on her oldest son with a hard expression. "I am. We will discuss your behavior later."

Lyle's face reddened. By simply witnessing the rebuke, Harrison had deepened the enmity there. With a last, hate-filled glare, Lyle turned and strode away.

Jamie broke the silence. "Mrs. DiMarko, we really need to speak with your husband."

"I'm sorry. That isn't possible right now. Victor is indisposed. Perhaps I can help you. Please sit down. You can't go anywhere until this wretched weather has passed. The radio reports it could be quite severe."

For a moment, Harrison thought Jamie was going to refuse. She looked to him. He inclined his head, holding out a chair for Iris at the nearest small table.

"I don't believe you've met your half sister, Fay."

"Hello, Fay."

The younger woman nodded as she took a seat. Her expression was impossible to decipher. Harrison couldn't tell if she was puzzled, shocked, angry, interested or bored meeting him. Jamie's features were less inscrutable. She was worried.

An abrupt flare of lightning and the immediate clash of thunder made her jump. Fat drops of rain began to splat against the windows.

"We had to rush to make it inside before the storm arrived," Iris continued.

The implication being that Iris DiMarko did not like to rush. Before he could respond, the woman who had been behind the bar appeared carrying a tray. Carefully, she set out four cups of coffee and plates of pastry.

"Thank you, Jill, that will be all for now."

"Yes, Mrs. DiMarko."

"Do try the napoleons, Harrison. Our pastry chef, Nico, is simply amazing." She lifted her cup and took a sip. No one else reached for the confections or their cups.

Harrison was used to reading people. He could generally tell a great deal from body language alone, but his father's wife stumped him. He couldn't tell if her genial demeanor was phony or genuine.

Fay's expression also remained blank. She sat stiffly without saying a word.

Jamie didn't pull her chair up to the table. She sat forward as if ready to spring up at a moment's notice—or to go for one of the weapons strapped to her body.

He let none of his own apprehension show, sitting back and crossing his legs. "Thank you, Iris. I'm really not hungry at the moment."

"Too bad, they are quite good. So, how may I help you, Harrison?"

"You could let your husband know we need to see him."

She shook her head regretfully. "I really can't. Your father has been ill, I'm afraid. He isn't seeing anyone."

"I understand, but we wouldn't have come if it wasn't urgent."

"Yes, I can believe that." She offered him a half smile to take the barb out of her words. "I know he's tried to speak with you several times."

Harrison nodded. He would not let her put

him on the defensive. After a second, she turned to Jamie.

"How are your foster parents, dear?"

"Dead."

The blunt word landed amid an enormous explosion of thunder. Every light in the place winked out.

For dramatic effect, the timing couldn't have been better. Either Fay or her mother inhaled sharply. He couldn't tell if it was in reaction to Jamie's response or the abrupt, all-consuming darkness that settled over the room.

Hairs rose along the back of his neck. A chair scraped back. He sensed Jamie rising to her feet. He stood as well. There was a decisive clink as Iris set down her coffee cup.

"Please. There's no need to be alarmed. I did say it was supposed to be a bad storm. Someone will be along with a flashlight shortly. If anyone has a lighter, we do have candles on all the tables."

Lightning streamed across the sky outside.

Harrison's eyes struggled to adjust. Jamie stood a few feet from their table, positioned with a solid wall to her back and what would have been a clear view of the rest of the room if there had been enough light to see by. Harrison was relieved that she wasn't holding a weapon, although he had no doubt she could have one in her hands in seconds.

The man called Arturo appeared with a small pocket flashlight and a lighter. No one spoke as he lit one candle after another on the tables scattered about the bar. The bartender followed him into the room. She set a lantern-style flashlight on one end of the bar.

"Please, won't you both sit back down?" Iris asked. "I'd like to hear what happened to Carolyn and Tony. Was it a car accident?"

JAMIE GLANCED AT HARRISON before lowering her gaze to Iris DiMarko. "No. They were murdered this morning."

The woman's eyes widened. She appeared to be shocked, but Jamie didn't know her well enough to determine whether the reaction was faked or genuine.

"No wonder you want to speak with Victor. I'm so sorry, Jamie. What an awful thing. They worked for us for so many years. They were like extended family." She turned to Harrison. "I believe Carolyn and your mother were close friends as well. It must have been a terrible shock for you both. Please, sit down for a moment."

Stunned, Jamie gaped at Harrison. He'd known Carolyn and he hadn't said anything?

His posture was rigid and Jamie realized he was coldly furious. Because Iris had revealed that connection, or because she knew of the association between his mother and her foster mother? His gaze was apologetic, but there was also a warning in the look he gave her.

"Sit down, Jamie."

Harrison's words were quietly spoken. He didn't look at her but waited with the outward calm and expectation of one who was used to being obeyed. Jamie was starting to know him.

He covered his tension well, but it was there in a dozen small tells she'd come to recognize. That was the only reason she didn't tell him where to stuff his order.

"Is something wrong?" Iris asked, gazing from one to the other.

Fay was also watching them with the first signs of interest that she had shown so far.

"Jamie doesn't like storms," he told them without a flicker in her direction.

"I don't like storms much myself," Iris agreed, "but we're perfectly safe in here. Please sit down, both of you. It's uncomfortable staring up at you."

Swallowing her inner turmoil, Jamie perched on the edge of her chair. Why hadn't Harrison told her? What else was he holding back?

Harrison resumed his chair, but this time he didn't settle back into the seat, either. And he kept his gaze averted. Still, Jamie watched him for cues.

Iris gave her bodyguard and the bartender a

pointed stare. Both turned and disappeared once more.

Iris smiled at Harrison and Jamie and lifted her cup. "Thank you. What I have to tell you is for your ears only."

Harrison appeared perfectly calm. Jamie hoped her own expression was now as unrevealing as his.

Iris lowered her voice. "Victor is quite ill."

"Mother!"

The protest was the first sound Fay had uttered. Her voice was low like her mother's but with a husky timbre.

"It's all right, dear. Harrison is family. They need to understand." Iris's gaze slid to him. "No one outside of the immediate family knows how bad the situation is. Harrison, your father is dying of pancreatic cancer. It's a matter of weeks, a month at the most. I know he would like very much to meet you. His mind is still strong, although he spends much of his time sleeping."

Jamie couldn't tell what Harrison thought of

that news, but the hairs along the back of her neck stood straight up.

"I'm sorry to hear that." His voice was low, again without enough inflection to tell her what he was thinking. "But that's all the more reason we need to speak with him as soon as possible. I wouldn't ask if this wasn't very important."

Iris was easy to read. She wanted to say no, yet she was clearly torn.

"Mother," Fay inserted. "You know Daddy isn't up to company."

Iris regarded her daughter blankly as if she'd forgotten her presence. A small frown marred the perfection of her face. "That's true, but he's wanted to meet Harrison for some time. He'd be very upset if he learned we turned him away."

Her decision made, she turned to Harrison, once more in command. "We're having a gathering this evening at the house. Victor is hoping to be well enough to attend, if only for a short time. Why don't you both come? The party starts at eight. You could spend the night."

Alarm rippled through Jamie. "No."

Harrison didn't lose a beat. Without glancing at her, he shook his head. "We appreciate the offer, Iris, but we don't want to crash a party and we certainly can't spend the entire night."

"Of course you must come." Iris spread her hands. "It's Gordon's birthday. There will be a large crowd and you'll have an opportunity to get to know your siblings."

She ignored Fay's dark scowl. "Really, there's no other way. We can't predict from minute to minute when Victor will feel up to visitors, but I know he'll come down for at least a short time. Although…" She paused as if considering. "He had a terribly rough morning today. It is possible he could sleep through the night. That's why you simply must stay at the house. You'll be available when he *can* see you. We have plenty of room. The house is the size of a small hotel." She turned to Jamie then. "And really, you shouldn't be alone at a time like this."

Jamie inclined her head in Harrison's direction without looking at him. "I'm not alone."

"No, of course not. I can see that you're friends. But we considered Carolyn and Tony family as well. They'd expect us to look out for you. Please. I insist you both come. You can even ride back to the house with Fay and me. It really would be good for your siblings to get to know you, Harrison."

Jamie spoke without thinking. "I take it you have a boxing ring where they can go ten rounds without breaking up the furniture."

Iris blinked in surprise, but Jamie sensed Harrison's smile.

"I must apologize for Lyle. As my oldest child, he tends to be unnecessarily protective of us, especially me. Victor and I have been married for thirty-eight years. I've raised my children to believe in the sanctity of marriage, so Lyle took his father's little indiscretion as an insult to me. I came to terms with his infidelity a long time ago. We were having problems at the time, and I understand that it didn't mean anything to him."

Harrison went very, very still.

"Oh. I'm sorry, dear. I meant no offense to your mother. I'm certain their time together meant a great deal to her, but unfortunately, Victor didn't view his liaisons the same way."

"You mean I'm not his only bastard?"

His voice was dangerously soft. This time the hairs rose along Jamie's arms as well as her neck. Harrison was coldly, deadly furious.

"No, no. After he learned about you, Victor had a vasectomy. I'm sorry. I'm handling this poorly. I just wanted you to understand why Lyle overreacted. It wasn't personal."

"You're mistaken."

Jamie braced herself to move quickly.

Iris appeared unfazed. "I'll speak with him."

"There's no need to do that on my account."

"Of course there is. He's your brother."

Implying they were all one big happy family? Who was she trying to kid? Iris moved on as if everything were settled.

"I'll have Arturo bring the car around."

"We have a car," Jamie told her.

"Oh, you can leave it in the lot. It will be safe here. Arturo can bring you back when you leave."

"There's no reason to put anyone to so much bother," Harrison told her smoothly. "If we're going to attend a party, we'll need to run a few errands first." He stood, concluding the subject.

Jamie hoped her relief didn't show. Iris didn't like being thwarted, but the flash of annoyance was quickly masked.

"Very well. I'll leave word at the gate to add you to the visitor list. But surely you aren't leaving now. At least wait for the storm to pass."

"We don't have a lot of time, Iris. A little rain won't hurt us."

"A LITTLE RAIN? Did you even look out here? We might drown if we aren't struck by lightning first," Jamie muttered as they made a dash for the car minutes later.

"Cheer up. The storm is slowing."

"Prove it."

He flashed her a reckless grin that took years off his features. "You look cute with your hair all plastered against your scalp like that."

No one had ever called her cute and her expression must have reflected that because his grin widened.

Jamie understood. She also felt relieved that they'd left the restaurant unscathed. The tension of the past few minutes had been far worse than she'd expected.

"Lyle's a dangerous enemy," she pointed out as they climbed into the car blinking rain from their eyes and cheeks.

"They all are. You don't have to go to the house with me, Jamie. Your promise to Tony only extended until noon. It's long past that now."

She wondered if she'd ever stop seeing their dead bodies in her mind. "This is personal."

"For both of us," he agreed.

"You owe me an explanation. Why you didn't tell me you knew Carolyn?"

"Frankly, it came as a pretty big shock to me as well. We were a bit pressed for a lengthy conversation at the time."

"We've been together for hours since then."

"True. But before you go all G.I. Jamie on me, try looking at it from my perspective."

"G.I. Jamie?"

He ignored that and held her gaze. "I didn't know you, Jamie. I was punchy from being drugged, sleep-deprived and I hadn't seen Ceecee since I was fourteen years old. My mother's best friend is lying there dead on the floor and you tell me she's the closest thing you have to a mother. What was I supposed to think?"

While his voice remained calm, the vein in his neck told her it was a surface calm only.

"In many ways, Ceecee was the last link I had to my mother's past. And then you hit me with the fact that she worked for my biological father." His jaw tightened. "I was supposed to get married today. And while you were kidnapping me last night, two thugs tried to take Zoe."

"The police cars at her apartment."

"Yes. I promised to protect her. Right now I'm afraid to go near her for fear of making the situation worse because I don't know what the situation is. When you come right down to it, I don't owe you anything, Jamie."

She swallowed hard. "No, you don't."

His tone and his body softened. "But we've got a common goal now. We both want answers and we need to stay alive if we're going to get the person responsible for killing Ceecee and her husband."

Silence filled the car. The rain was the only sound.

"I need to run home and pick up some clothing," he said finally.

The tension drained out of her. She started the engine. "Funny man. Remember the people out there who want to kill you?"

"I thought we just left them."

She nearly smiled at his attempted levity. "Maybe we did, but your place is out of the question. If you need something, we stop and buy it. We don't make it easy for the killers and hard for me."

"Still trying to guard my body?"

Her lips did quirk then. "I've had worse assignments."

"That right? Name two."

"The old man with the hairpiece that kept slipping and the woman who wanted me to wear a gun strapped to my leg like some Wild West gunslinger."

He laughed out loud. "You made that up."

"Maybe." It was fun to banter with him, easing away the tension of the past few hours.

"Do you lead when you dance, too?"

"I don't dance."

"We'll have to correct that."

His voice was low and far too intimate for comfort. Her stomach gave a funny twist and roll. "Men like you shouldn't flirt with the hired help."

His sudden stillness was alarming. "I never hired you."

"Good point."

He watched her with an intensity that made her want to squirm. "What did you mean by 'men like me'?"

She cursed her stupidity. "You're wealthy."

"That isn't generally listed in the minus column."

"Depends on who's doing the listing."

"Okay, I feel like I zoned out for part of this conversation. Please explain."

She didn't want to. The conversation had veered into an uncomfortable area. Time to bring things back on track right now.

"We're from different worlds, Harrison." She raised a hand when he would have objected. "And before we get into another pointless discussion, do you have a place you want to go for whatever clothes you think you need for this evening?"

She didn't think he was going to let it slide. For a second, she was pretty sure neither did he.

"This discussion isn't over, Jamie."

Her body hummed at the warning, but when she didn't respond, he gave her directions to an exclusive men's shop. It was still raining, so they looked like a pair of bedraggled refugees when they stepped inside the carpet-lined display room. Nevertheless, his appearance didn't detract a whit from the aura of command he projected. Jamie was impressed. In less than ten minutes he had two clerks all but falling over themselves to help him select an entire wardrobe including a suit and a very expensive handmade Italian tie that they agreed to wrap as a gift for Gordon.

"It's a birthday party," he told her when she raised her eyebrows. "We should probably pick up a card as well."

Jamie was still reeling when they left the store. In a short space of time Harrison had managed to come perilously close to maxing out her credit card. She could hardly complain, since his wallet was at the Van Wheeler estate where she'd left it.

"I'll reimburse you," he promised as he held the large umbrella over her head until she was back in the car.

"With interest," she agreed dryly as he slipped in beside her.

"We should stop and get a dress for you. I have a feeling this party will be formal."

"Don't worry about it. I'm your bodyguard, not your date. They'll deal."

"Trust me, you'll be more comfortable if you blend in. You're a beautiful woman, Jamie. You don't need to hide your curves beneath loose-fitting tops."

"No, I need to hide my gun. *You* trust *me*. There's no way I'd ever blend in with those people even in a designer original."

"Those *people* are related to me," he reminded her softly, "however regrettable that may be."

"You have my sympathy."

"Are you always this contrary?"

"Only Saturdays through Sunday."

That netted her a full smile. He had such a terrific smile. Charm, she reminded herself sternly, was part of Harrison's stock in trade. And he probably came by it genetically if what his stepmother said was true.

"Okay to head back to the motel?" she asked. "I'd like to get into some dry clothing myself."

"Sure you don't want to stop somewhere? I'd like to buy you something special."

"Thanks all the same, but I'm sure."

Harrison settled back. "What was your take on the scene at the restaurant?"

Wryly, she raised her eyebrows. "Which scene?"

"Let's start with Lyle."

"Lyle's a puffer fish, swelled with his own importance. I'm sure he can be dangerous, but the one you'd better watch is his mother."

"Iris is definitely the one in control," he agreed.

"And *she* has the most reason to hate you."

"I just met the woman. It generally takes a day at least to raise the level to hate."

"I'm not joking, Harrison. When your father dies you might want to request an autopsy. Black widows generally kill their mates."

He sucked in a breath. "That's pretty harsh."

"Maybe. But Iris didn't ask the right questions. She should have asked how and why we came to be together."

"You think we make such an odd couple?"

"Yes." She stated it flatly. "Iris would see only one reason someone like me would be with someone like you. I'm a professional bodyguard. I'm sure she knows that. She must also know I work out of L.A., not Virginia, yet she didn't question why we were together."

"We could have met socially."

She shot him a quelling stare. "No. We couldn't have."

That raised his eyebrows. "Because I'm not your type?"

"Because I don't date men out of my socio-economic bracket."

"Ouch."

"I'd think you'd understand. You were born because your mother didn't follow that rule." She'd stepped over the line, but she wasn't sorry. "Should I apologize?"

"Not for stating the truth."

A glance at his features gave her no clues to his thoughts. "Why are we having this conversation? You asked for my opinion of the scene at the restaurant. My opinion is that we walked into a snake pit without antivenom."

"Spiders and vipers. I thought you said Tony and Carolyn liked them."

"They did. I didn't say *I* did." Grief shrouded her heart once more. She forced the pain down.

"The DiMarkos could be innocent, Jamie."

"And the earth could be flat. They may not have arranged for Tony and Carolyn's murder, but the DiMarkos are *not* innocent. You know that."

"Neither were Tony and Carolyn, not if they worked for the family."

She bristled, even knowing he was right.

"We don't know who asked Tony for the favor. It could have been Ceecee herself."

A driver cut her off, giving Jamie a reason to swear. Lightning skittered across the sky in the distance.

"Why?" she demanded. "What reason would she have?"

"I've no idea. If I go by my memories of her, I'd have to say she wanted to protect me for some reason. And whoever she was protecting me from found out and attempted to kill me anyhow."

Jamie knew it was possible.

"And we can't overlook the fact that someone tried to take Zoe last night. I told you the man she once dated was gunned down beside her last week."

Jamie waited for the rumble of thunder to die down. "How is that related?"

"I have no idea, but it would be a strange coincidence if the events weren't connected somehow, don't you think?"

Jamie considered that and sighed. "We don't know enough yet."

"I agree."

They fell silent as she turned her attention to the busy streets. "Did you notice that Iris sent everyone out of the room before she told you that your father is dying?"

Harrison frowned. "Yes. So?"

"So she said only the immediate family knows Victor is dying."

It took him almost a full minute. "You aren't family."

Chapter Six

"Maybe you shouldn't go with me tonight," Harrison suggested.

"Try to stop me."

"I would, but I don't have a battalion handy."

Trying not to smile, she glanced at him and he winked. Why couldn't he have been old or ugly?

She turned her attention back to the road in time to avert a collision with a large SUV. "Oops."

"Let's not do our enemy's job for them."

"It wasn't that close."

There was a smile in his voice. "I don't want to know what you'd call close, then."

"Why do you call Carolyn 'Ceecee'?"

"It's the only name I've ever known her by." He rubbed his temple.

"Headache?"

He nodded.

"You're tired."

"We both are, Jamie."

"True enough. Do you think Iris was telling the truth?"

"Which truth?"

Jamie picked her words carefully. "If Victor DiMarko is dying of cancer, what are the odds she'll let us see him?"

"Why wouldn't she?"

"You saw her reaction. She wanted to agree with Fay, but I think she's afraid of her husband."

Harrison was paying close attention.

"Victor DiMarko built himself an empire," Jamie continued. "Who stands to inherit when he dies? Do you think hot-tempered Lyle could run things?"

"Probably not for long," he admitted.

"Shy, quiet Fay? Baby brother Gordon?"

Jamie shook her head dismissively. "Iris is in charge. I have a suspicion she likes that position."

"You may be right, but what does that have to do with her letting us see him?"

"I think they're all worried that Victor has another successor in mind. One with savvy business skills and all sorts of untapped potential."

Her words found their target.

"You said it yourself, he's been trying to bring you into the fold."

She'd jolted him, but the more the words settled, the more it felt right. "You think Iris wants me out of the way."

"I would."

"What about the attempts on Zoe?"

Jamie chose her words with care. "She's pregnant with another potential usurper. Get rid of your whole line and problem solved. Down the road Lyle might give Iris a run for her money, but for now, having a loose cannon would make a convenient scapegoat if she needed one."

Harrison's gaze bored into her. "You're down-right scary, you know that?"

"Thank you. Do you think I'm right?"

"It's definitely something to consider."

He fell silent for several minutes. "How did you end up in the military?"

The question surprised her. There was no reason not to answer, so she shrugged. "I wanted money for college. Carolyn and Tony offered to pay my way, but they'd done enough so I enlisted."

"Accepting help doesn't make a person weak, Jamie."

"You'd have done the same as me and we both know it. I'm not a helpless female, Harrison. I prefer to meet the world on my terms."

"That's one of the many things I admire about you. But I'd like five minutes with the guy who made you feel that was your only option."

Jamie was stunned by the hard edge to those words. Harrison saw entirely too much. She pulled into the parking lot of the motel and shut off the engine. Neither of them made any move to get out of the car.

"He's dead," she surprised herself by admitting.

"Did you kill him?"

Shocked, she turned to face him. There was no censure in his expression, only sympathy.

"No. My stepfather beat my mother one time too many. She finally got the courage to use his forty-five on him before she turned it on herself. Satisfied?"

"Not at all. He got off too easy."

She swallowed hard. "Yes. He did."

She climbed out of the car before he could say anything more. Any show of sympathy would have undone her completely. She was under better control by the time she got the door open.

"We need to take some precautions tonight," she told him as he carried his purchases inside and set them on the nearest chair.

"What do you suggest?"

She thought through her answer carefully.

"Don't let anyone isolate you. Watch what you eat and drink."

He smiled. "You think someone might poison me?"

"There are a lot of things besides poison that can be slipped into foods and drinks."

"I'll let you sample everything first," he promised.

"I'm a bodyguard, not a food taster. You asked for my opinion."

"So I did. Sorry, continue."

"Eat only what everyone else does and never let your drink out of your sight. Once it escapes your notice, don't touch it again. Stay near people at all times. The more the better. It's not likely she'll risk a scene in front of company, but if one of them gets you isolated, bear in mind that the DiMarkos know how to make people disappear."

Her cautions might be a little over-the-top, but sobered, Harrison nodded. Blowing up a farmhouse with four people inside was pretty over-the-top as well.

Jamie yawned.

"A nap would be good about now," he commented.

"There isn't time. We should probably get something to eat before we have to leave."

"There's a sub place right down the street. You could lie down while I go pick something up."

"We'll both go."

He cocked his head. "You don't trust me?"

"Strangely enough, I do."

Satisfied, he touched her arm lightly. "Let's go get something to eat."

They picked up soup, subs and a newspaper and took everything back to the motel, where they shared the paper along with their meal. Jamie picked at her food, eating only a portion of the generous sub. But she drank most of the pot of coffee she brewed to go with the meal.

"You're going to spend the entire night in the bathroom," he warned.

"No. I'm two parts camel."

"Would the other parts be mule?"

Her eyes twinkled, despite the exhaustion he knew they both felt. "Quite possibly. I'm going to take another shower and get ready."

She stretched, bending and twisting to loosen tired muscles. His gaze riveted on her slim figure, and a deep sense of anticipation stirred. He didn't want this strong pull of attraction. If things had gone differently he'd have married Zoe this morning.

But he hadn't.

Despite all his pragmatism, the possibility that he or Zoe might one day meet someone who would hold more than a physical attraction for them had seemed abstract and unlikely. At least on his part. He'd dated extensively without ever finding someone he was deeply drawn to.

Zoe had seemed like the answer. They would marry, give her child a name, raise it and continue on as they always had, the best of friends and working partners. The only change in status would be living together and sharing a bedroom.

Only he didn't want to share a bed with Zoe, and he badly wanted to share one with Jamie.

She caught him staring and straightened quickly. "Something wrong?"

"The list keeps growing."

Her eyes narrowed. "If you're going where I think you are with that, you can stop right there."

"That's definitely my plan," he agreed wryly. "However, after I speak with Zoe, all bets are off."

Her heart began to thud wildly. "Forget it, Harrison."

"Not going to happen, Jamie. You're impossible to forget."

"We are not having this conversation."

"You feel the attraction the same as I do."

"No."

"Look me in the eye and say that."

She turned for the bedroom. "Do you want to use the bathroom first?"

"Put up all the walls you want. When the dust settles we'll have this conversation again."

Badly rattled, she shook her head. "In your dreams."

"Undoubtedly. I'll dress in here." He nodded toward where he'd left the new clothing on the chair.

Quaking inside, Jamie disappeared into the bedroom, closing the connecting panels with hands that were none too steady. She would not let him get to her like this. Harrison Trent was just used to women falling at his feet. She was a challenge, nothing more. Jamie had dealt with men like him before.

Liar, her brain cried out. She'd never known anyone like Harrison Trent.

"GOOD JOB, HARRISON," he told his reflection in the mirror over the small table. "A little sleep deprivation and you send her running." What she didn't understand was that he'd spooked them both with the depth of his growing hunger for her.

"Definitely sleep-deprived."

Pacing the room, he decided to seize the opportunity to give Artie another call.

"Harrison? Where *are* you?"

"Preparing to beard a lion in its den. Have you talked to Zoe?"

"Not since this morning, but the police want to talk to both of you. I don't know what Carter told them, but they aren't happy. What's going on?"

"I'm working on that. Someone wants me dead."

"Go figure."

Harrison found he could smile after all. "I have a bodyguard who's trying to prevent it from happening."

"Yeah? Not one of Ramsey's people. They're looking for you as well. I was about to call Ramsey. I'm at your place right now. I came over to see if I could find Leon's number. I thought I should let him know what's going on. Not that I *know* what's going on."

"That makes two of us."

Harrison's friend, housekeeper and former pro footballer often served as his unofficial bodyguard. But Leon's mother had been rushed into surgery on Wednesday. Harrison had chartered a private jet and driven him to the airport.

"Don't call him, Artie. He has enough on his plate right now. His mom is really ill."

"Okay, but look, someone's been in here. Tell me it wasn't you."

"What are you talking about?"

"There's a first aid kit in the downstairs bathroom. A man's bloody shirt is in the wastebasket."

Harrison inhaled sharply.

"I'm guessing the bodyguard was injured and Zoe cleaned him up. It looks like she changed clothes. The spare bedroom's been rifled, but it wasn't a thief. I'm standing here holding a great big hunking diamond ring. The one Drake gave Zoe, I think. You both have better taste than this. I tried calling Zoe but her cell phone's turned off. I didn't leave a message."

"Call Ramsey, Artie. See if he can find Zoe."

"What about you?"

"I'd as soon no one found me right now."

Ramsey and his people were good, but Harrison didn't want to pit them against his father's organized crime syndicate.

"Can you see to it Zoe is protected until I find out how everything is linked?"

"You know I will. Talk to me. What do you need?"

Harrison hesitated. Was it worth putting his friend in danger? "No. It's not worth the risk."

"English, Harrison. What isn't worth the risk?"

He rubbed at his jaw, weighing the odds. "I need my wallet, cell phone and suitcase."

"I'll bring them."

"I was going to ask you, but it's too risky. Someone might follow you."

"They can try."

Artie's voice roughened in a way Harrison had heard only once or twice before. The two of them went back several years now. People tended to underestimate Artie. Harrison knew how hard he worked at his carefree, playboy image. Few saw beneath that exterior.

"Four people are dead, Artie. Someone doesn't care about collateral damage."

"Got it. I'll be careful. Does this go back to Zoe's connection to Drake?"

"Maybe. I'm not sure yet."

"Okay. The police have your cell phone, but I can bring the rest. Where and when?"

Jamie would have a conniption if he met Artie here. "How about the parking lot of the Reston Motor Lodge and Conference Center?"

"Where we met Armstead last week? Parking will be tight on a Saturday night."

"I'm counting on it."

Artie sensed his friend's feral smile. "What time?"

It would mean driving in the opposite direction of where they had to go, but it would also give them plenty of room to spot tails.

"Can you make it there by seven-thirty?"

"Yes."

"Watch your back, Artie."

"Always."

Disconnecting, Harrison glanced at the clock. There was no sound of the shower running and no noise coming from the bedroom beyond the closed panel doors. He'd have to get dressed if he wanted to be ready when she was.

He was straightening his tie in the small mirror when the bedroom panel slid back. Clamping down on his eager senses, he turned slowly and felt as if he'd taken a visceral blow to his midsection.

Jamie's wild, spiky hair shimmered in a softly tamed halo about her face and head. Understated makeup had been deftly applied. A soft, black shimmery material skimmed her trim form from her neck to her ankles, leaving her arms and shoulders bare.

As she took a gliding step forward, Harrison realized what he'd taken to be a full-length evening gown was actually wide-legged pants that allowed freedom of movement. The matching black halter top, so demure in front, bared most of her delicate back. Long crystal earrings swung gaily as she moved, glittering like the silver chain she dangled in one hand that had a small black evening bag on the other end. She carried a matching black jacket in her other hand.

She looked delicate and exotic. His body stirred in immediate reaction. "Wow."

Feminine satisfaction curved her lips. "Still worried I won't blend in?"

"You won't. You'll put the other women to shame."

"Thank you. Are you all set?"

"I am now."

She turned away to set the purse on the counter so she could put on the jacket. He spanned the distance in a single stride and took the jacket from her fingers. A small shiver went through her as their hands brushed.

"Allow me."

"I can do it."

"I'm certain you can do almost anything, but my mother raised me to be a gentleman."

"I'm your bodyguard," she reminded him.

He smiled. "You're the one who needs a bodyguard tonight."

She turned to face him. "I'm immune to flattery, Mr. Trent."

Unable to resist, he brushed his knuckle against her cheek. "Liar."

The whispered word mingled with the desire tightening his body. Her eyes sparked with matching awareness, masked instantly by caution. "I don't get involved with my clients."

"No problem. You're fired."

She shook her head. "You didn't hire me in the first place."

"Then we don't have a problem, do we?"

She took in a shuddery breath. "I'm starting to think we have a big problem."

Harrison took a reluctant step back before he did something irreversible, like touch her again.

"You could be right. We're going to have a full agenda with all the items we're tabling for now."

The downward sweep of her lashes masked her eyes.

"But if we don't leave right now," he told her gently, resisting the impulse to touch her once again, "we aren't going to leave for a long time."

Her eyes flashed open. "I'm not that easy."

"I am."

JAMIE WAS GLAD for the protection afforded by the umbrella. She did not want to be attracted to Harrison Trent. Her policy of never getting involved with the people she protected was firm. Even if it hadn't been, his bride-to-be was pregnant. Harrison Trent was off-limits in all caps.

She never let anyone get close enough to hurt her. How was it Harrison seemed to be slipping past her defenses so easily? She couldn't allow that to happen.

"We're going to be early," she warned him, pleased that her voice didn't reveal her inner turmoil because Tony's car suddenly seemed smaller and far more intimate than it had been before.

"Actually, we're going to be fashionably late. We need to make a quick stop in Reston."

She snapped around to face him. "Who did you call?"

"Artie. He's going to meet us with my wallet and bag."

Her soft oath was heartfelt. "If you have some sort of secret death wish, tell me now."

"We can trust him."

"Can we also trust the cops or killers who might follow him to this meeting?"

"He won't be followed."

"You're betting both our lives on that."

"It's okay, Jamie. Trust him. Trust *me*." He held her gaze. "We have to trust someone."

"No. We don't! If you get us both killed, I'm going to haunt you for eternity."

"You mentioned that before. But after seeing you in that outfit, I don't think death is going to be required."

"Stop that!"

"Stop what?"

She turned away fuming and squished the secret part of her that warmed to his words. She never let a man get to her like this. She never let *anyone* get to her like this!

"There's limited parking, Jamie. If someone does manage to follow Artie, they're going to stand out. He isn't as foolish as you might believe."

"Van Wheeler didn't strike me as foolish in any way. He came to the kitchen and instructed the help personally right before your party. A foolish man would have left that to his housekeeper."

"That's Artie."

Van Wheeler had made her nervous at the time even though his voice and manner had seemed relaxed and easygoing. Jamie had sensed then that he was not a person to underestimate. She'd been told he came from inherited wealth and had amassed even more. He and Trent had been college roommates. Tony told her they collaborated frequently on large undertakings.

"He'll recognize me."

"So what? Jamie, by now both our pictures are probably news. We both know we're on borrowed time."

Jamie changed tactics. "Does your *friend* stand to profit from your sudden demise?"

She sensed his shock without looking. But there was amusement in his voice when he responded.

"No. Artie could buy and sell me without raising a sweat. He's one of the few people I trust completely. Who do you trust, Jamie?"

She risked meeting his eyes. "No one."

"I'm sorry. You must be very lonely."

A barely contained swell of grief ambushed her from nowhere at his softly spoken words. Carolyn and Tony were dead. She was all alone once more.

Jamie was grateful for the heavy traffic. She couldn't afford to go all weepy. She needed to stay focused. "I need directions," she told him gruffly. To her profound relief, he gave them without saying more.

Traffic was slow. Headlights threw up a terrible glare from the rain-slicked pavement. The glare was giving her a headache. She hoped she could find some caffeine when they arrived at the party.

Harrison didn't break the silence again until they approached the parking lot of the sprawling complex. "Pull around to the back where the conference center is. Artie will park in one of the handicapped spots near the door."

"Good way to draw police attention."

"We won't be here that long. If you pull in front of his car, I'll get out and take the bag from him and we'll drive away."

"*You'll* stay in the car. *I'll* take the bag from him."

"He's not going to shoot me, Jamie."

"I might. This isn't open for arbitration. We do this my way. You can wave at him from inside the car. Once you climb out you're a clear target for anyone with a rifle scope."

"So are you."

"That doesn't matter."

"It does to me."

He sounded so sincere. Tears threatened her composure. "Stop saying things like that!"

"Not going to happen. Artie came because I asked him to. We're all at risk. This is my turn." He smiled as if to take some of the sting from his words. "Besides, you'll get wet."

"Better than you getting dead."

Without warning, he unbuckled his seat belt, leaned over and kissed her cheek. Then he pointed toward the rear entrance. "That's his Lamborghini."

The sporty red car squatted before the handicapped sign as if daring anyone to challenge its right to park there or anywhere else it wanted. Jamie pulled up, penning the small car in place with the rear of hers, and popped the trunk. Harrison flung open his door and stepped from the car.

Jamie cursed silently, her gaze sweeping the wet parking lot fearfully. The storm was gathering force for another strike.

Harrison moved forward as Artie stepped from his car and paused to haul Harrison's suitcase from the passenger's seat. Artie clapped Harrison on the shoulder. "Glad to see you in one piece."

"Thanks. The feeling's mutual."

Harrison tossed the bag into the open trunk. Artie handed him his wallet and keys as a jagged spear of lightning crossed the sky. Artie nodded at Jamie. "How is it you always get the girl?"

"I don't have this one yet."

Artie's head swiveled back to face him and his eyes narrowed. "I know her. She was the tall bartender last night."

"Side job." Harrison slammed the trunk closed. "Do you know what you're doing?"

"At the moment, trying to stay alive. Jamie's a professional, Artie. She's already saved my life once. I trust her."

"What about Zoe? If you leave her hanging, I'll marry her myself."

"She won't have you, but I appreciate the thought."

Artie swore. "I told you the marriage was a bad idea."

"Noted. Zoe's my friend."

"She's my friend, too. That's why I knew it was a mistake. You're going to hurt her."

"No."

They stared at each other for a bleak moment.

"I took Zoe's ring home and put it in my safe. I know you think the penthouse is impregnable, but leaving something like that sitting out is just asking for trouble." Van Wheeler looked past Harrison to lock eyes with Jamie. She'd rolled down the window to glare at them. "Take care of him. I intend to beat him to a pulp later on."

"Sounds good. I'll help. Let's go, Harrison."

Slapping the roof of the car, Artie stepped back. Harrison climbed back in and Jamie put the car in gear and peeled out of the lot accompanied by a new roar of thunder. Harrison belted himself in.

She didn't say anything, but neither of them relaxed until they were back on the main road.

"No one shot at us," he pointed out.

"And we haven't blown up."

"Blown up?"

"Anything could have been inside that bag he tossed in the trunk."

"You cannot be serious."

"You're too trusting."

"And you don't trust at all. Some things you have to take on faith, Jamie."

"That's what martyrs always say. You'll note they usually end up dead. I'm trying to keep you alive. It would help if you'd stop making my job so difficult."

Harrison shook his head. "How did you get into bodyguarding in the first place?"

"It's what I always wanted to do."

"Why?"

"Protecting people is important."

Harrison studied her expression. "Because someone didn't protect you when it was important?" Her flinch was barely perceptible, but telling.

"We should figure out a contingency plan for tonight in case something goes wrong."

"Like what?" He let her change the subject. Jamie had obviously built her walls of necessity. She wasn't going to willingly let them crumble. He'd have to pick away at the weak spots little by little.

She scowled in his direction and he shrugged. "It's tough to plan when we have no idea what we're walking into."

"Trouble."

"You'll handle it."

Her scowl deepened. "I'm immune to flattery."

"Not flattery. I respect professionalism. I have a few trust issues myself."

At her skeptical look, he tipped his head to study her profile. "I was born a bastard, Jamie. It's more acceptable in today's world, but it still puts you on the outside in most situations. I know what it's like to shut away part of yourself so no one can get close. There's a measure of safety in that, but it can be lonely."

"Thank you, Dr. Freud."

Time to back off. "Nope. Freud was about id and ego. I'm curious as to how you became involved with Tony and Ceecee."

He expected her to ignore the question. When she began to answer, he had the sense that they were both surprised.

"I used to panhandle around a place where Tony often ate lunch. The manager offered me a job even though he knew I was underage. I think Tony suggested it. The two of them seemed very friendly. Tony showed up with Carolyn a few afternoons later. They offered me a place to stay on the condition I got my GED."

"You turned them down." At her look, he shrugged. "I would have. They could have been sexual predators."

Jamie relaxed. "I considered that. And you're right, I did turn them down. But when the cops rousted the underpass where a group of us were camped, I figured I didn't have much to lose. Looking back, I wonder if Tony didn't arrange that as well. It was turning winter and rain was predicted. I hate being cold and wet. Their offer looked better than a deserted doorway or one of those halfway houses."

"I'm glad they were there for you."

He should have known better than to offer sympathy. Her shields snapped into place right away.

"The world is full of runaways. I got lucky."

"You're right. Did your stepfather abuse you, Jamie?" But he'd pushed it too far.

"Enough true confessions for one night, unless *you* want to discuss how you feel about meeting your father face-to-face for the first time."

He let it go. "Touché. I'm not happy about it."

"Well, brace yourself, because this is our exit."

The lofty mansion towered behind a forbidding gated wall that would have given any intruder second thoughts even without all the visible high-tech security in place. Harrison eyed the grounds with distaste.

"It's not too late to change your mind," she told him as they waited for the Porsche in front of them to be passed through.

"Yes, it is."

They presented their drivers' licenses to a beefy guard who checked them against a roster before waving them through.

"See, I told you I needed my wallet. At least they didn't do a strip search."

"We aren't inside yet."

She stopped in front of the main entrance, where a wiry young man offered her the protection of an umbrella. Jamie wasn't happy when she realized she'd have to surrender the car to the valet, but short of making a scene, she had little choice.

"Not good," she muttered.

"I'm sure they'll be careful with Tony's car."

"Which will do us no good if we need to leave in a hurry."

"True, but I doubt the guard at the front gate would let us leave in a hurry anyhow if the DiMarkos wanted us to stay."

She glared at him. "That isn't inspiring any confidence here."

"We're agreed on that."

The front door opened and the couple before them were ushered inside. Gordon DiMarko greeted the couple cordially and after a few brief words sent them on their way.

There was nothing friendly in the look he turned on them. "Do you really think you're welcome here?"

"After such an effusive greeting? Happy birthday." Harrison handed him the wrapped tie.

His brother glared at the package and then at him. "What do you want from us?"

"Answers."

"And a place in Dad's organization?"

"No, thank you. I have an aversion to jail cells."

Jamie's "oh, boy" was soft. She tensed, but whatever reply Gordon wanted to make was swallowed as a pair of his boisterous friends arrived on their heels.

Harrison took Jamie's arm lightly, thanked the woman who took the dripping umbrella from his hand and moved past his brother.

The spacious foyer opened onto a large formal living room. People milled about in small groups, ignoring the antique furnishings, while waiters and waitresses moved around the room with trays of drinks and canapés. Harrison wasn't surprised when Jamie turned down an offer of wine. He did the same.

"Is it possible to get a soft drink?" Jamie asked the waiter.

"Yes, ma'am. There's a bar in the family room through there." He nodded to their left. "Or I could bring you something."

"We'll go through there, thank you."

They flowed in the indicated direction.

"No ice sculptures or crepe paper for Gordon," Harrison noted.

Jamie actually smiled. It was small, but it was the first real smile she'd ever offered him. Harrison wanted to see more.

"Those were pretty awful."

"Artie's got a weird sense of humor. But you have to admit a little crepe paper would go a long way to cheering this place up."

"What have you got against refined elegance?"

"Boredom?"

Her laugh was a low tinkling sound that curved his lips in answer. "Do you honestly think we'll be bored here tonight?"

"There you are, Gordon!" An emaciated woman weaved her way to his side sloshing a glass half-full of red wine. "Happa birshday."

"Lenore, that isn't Gordon." The man who took her arm had an apologetic expression.

"Course it is. Looks jush like his father. I need to pee. Where's the bathroom?"

"This way. I'm sorry. Excuse us." And he led the woman off.

"Bored yet?" Jamie asked, and elbowed her way to the bar without waiting for a response. "I don't suppose you have coffee."

"No, ma'am," the server replied. "Try the kitchen."

"Two colas, then. Whatever has the most caffeine."

Harrison watched Jamie watch the server pour the drinks. He was reminded of her earlier cautions. "This is going to be a long night."

"I hope not," she told him, handing him a glass and moving to allow a large man space at the bar.

"There's Fay." His half sister stood at the far end of the room with two men who looked like Hollywood versions of mobsters. The lights flickered as thunder rattled windowpanes.

"I hope omens don't bother you."

"Seems rather appropriate under the circumstances."

"What's he doing?"

Harrison followed her gaze to the bank of windows overlooking the rain-swept deck. Lyle towered menacingly over a slender young woman. She was all but pressed against the sliding glass door and she did not look as if she was enjoying the attention. Harrison thrust his glass at Jamie and cut a path through the crowd.

"How much money will it take?" Lyle was demanding.

The young woman thrust out her jaw. "You can't buy me off."

Lyle's hands fisted. Before he could bring up an arm, Harrison covered it with his hand. "You need to learn to control your temper, Lyle."

His brother whirled. "You!"

"Me," he agreed. "You seem to enjoy creating scenes. I doubt your mother will be happy if you slug this young woman or me in front of all these witnesses."

Lyle pulled free. "Get out of here."

"I was invited."

"So was I," the unknown woman said.

For a second Harrison thought Lyle was going to strike one of them anyhow.

"I'll deal with you later." He strode off, his florid features a mask of suppressed rage.

"He should have his blood pressure checked," Jamie murmured.

"He's a jerk." The woman followed him with watchful eyes before looking at the two of them. "Thanks for the rescue. I half expected him to shove me out on the deck."

"Or over it," Jamie agreed.

"There's a thought. I'm Elizabeth Sylor. Liz."

"Jamie Bellman. This is Harrison Trent."

Her eyes widened. "The bastard?"

Harrison raised his eyebrows. "Depends on if you mean that literally or have a bone to pick with me."

She flushed. "I'm sorry. That was rude. You're Gordon's half brother."

"Guilty."

"He keeps telling me I need to think before I speak."

"Generally sound advice," Harrison agreed. "I take it you know Gordon."

"He was planning to announce our engagement tonight."

From Jamie's expression, Harrison gathered he wasn't the only one surprised by her bald statement. "Lyle objects?"

"They all do." Her eyes flashed angrily. "We don't care."

"Why do they?" Jamie asked. "Are you the police chief's daughter?"

"District attorney's."

"Oh."

Amused, Harrison regarded her. "In that case I'd think it would be your family that objected."

"They do. I'm still going to marry him. My father wants to arrest Victor and Lyle, but Gordon isn't like them. He doesn't want to work in the family business. He wants to be an architect. He's got his degree and everything. He's terrific."

Remembering Gordon's greeting when he arrived, Harrison wasn't so sure Gordon didn't want to work in the family business, but he wasn't going to tell this little firebrand as much.

"Harrison!"

The sound of his name saved him from a reply. Iris DiMarko strode over to them like a queen. She looked striking in a deep red sheath and matching stiletto heels. More than one head turned as she passed.

She added a dismissive nod at Jamie and centered her attention on Harrison. "I'm glad you were able to come. I see you've met Gordon's *friend,* Elizabeth."

There was no missing her inflection on the word *friend.* It should have been preceded with the word *little.*

"Iris." Harrison returned the greeting.

"Is Victor ready to see us?" Jamie asked.

Iris's frown of irritation dissolved as quickly

as it appeared. "Not just yet." She glanced meaningfully at Liz. "Victor is tied up at the moment, but he does plan to be down in time to watch Gordon blow out the candles on his cake. Elizabeth, I believe Gordon was looking for you a few minutes ago in the living room."

With an *I told you so* look at Harrison, she sighed. "I'd better go and find him, then. Nice meeting you, Mr. Trent, Ms. Bellman. Thanks again."

Harrison watched her walk away. Her simple black dress was seriously understated in this crowd. "Nice young lady."

"Yes. Gordon has any number of nice friends. Please excuse me for a moment. Do avail yourselves of the buffet. If you need anything at all, just ask one of the staff."

She strode away, mission complete.

"What was that all about?" Jamie asked.

"I don't think she liked us fraternizing with another potential problem."

"She's probably concerned we'll spill damaging secrets that Liz could take home to Daddy."

Harrison smiled wryly. "Romeo and Juliet are alive and well. Maybe you should warn Liz about watching her drink."

"Maybe I should." Jamie followed Iris's progress through the room. "Let's do as she suggested and get something to eat while we can. We need sustenance to stay alert."

"I thought we weren't supposed to eat anything."

"Only items that other guests are eating. Nothing that is specially prepared for you."

"Got it." He followed her toward the crowded dining room. "Do you really think anyone will try something in this crush?"

"Lyle just did."

"Point to you, but I don't really think he'd have hit her."

"He'd have regretted it if he had. Daddy would have had him on assault and battery charges. On the other hand, it's a straight drop off that deck. You may have noticed this house is on a steep hillside. A person could get badly hurt if he slipped and fell over that railing."

"You're just full of cheery thoughts, aren't you?"

"Doing my job."

"Do you ever take time off?"

"Yes. I'm here in Virginia on vacation."

Ruefully, Harrison followed her lead as they took plates from the lavish spread and stood around nibbling on some excellent jumbo shrimp.

"I'll have to find out who did their catering," he told her. "This is quite good. Try a bite."

She gazed in surprise as he held out a shrimp for her to taste and lowered his voice so only Jamie could hear. "What do you think of our chances of getting upstairs and locating Victor before the cake is cut?"

Jamie masked her relief and nibbled on the shrimp, and Harrison knew for certain in that moment that he would not be marrying Zoe after all.

"What?"

He pressed his lips to her ear and felt her small shiver. "We have an audience."

She smiled brilliantly up at him. "Behave. I wonder who painted that watercolor."

Harrison pasted on a smile as if what had just transpired had been between two lovers. He followed her to the abstract painting on the wall. This put their backs to the crowd and the waiter who'd been watching them closely.

"The tuxedo-clad man at the bottom of the main staircase isn't a guest or there to take coats," Jamie told him softly. "There's probably a second man stationed up top in case he gets distracted."

Nodding as if she were talking about the painting, Harrison tipped his head and stared at it instead of looking at her. "A house this size must have another staircase."

"It does," she agreed in a normal tone before lowering her voice. "Off the kitchen filled with people in tuxedos."

"I'm impressed."

"I'm good at what I do."

His lips twisted wryly. "So you're saying the odds aren't good."

"Not without a distraction."

"What did you have in mind?"

Chapter Seven

Jamie nearly returned Harrison's smile. It wasn't fair that he was so handsome. "Let's move closer to the kitchen while I think about it."

"This contradicts staying with the crowd," he reminded her.

"I know, but there's an undercurrent in the air I don't like. See those two men over there?"

Harrison swept his gaze over the room in the right direction. "The ones Fay was talking with earlier? What about them?"

"Cheap suits for this crowd."

"Let's call the fashion police."

"They've been watching us and trying not to look like they're watching us. Mark the nearest exit and be ready in case we have to leave in a hurry."

Harrison blinked. "You think they're going to start something?"

"Probably not unless we give them an opening." She stopped beside a trio of women near the kitchen door without actually joining them. The location let Jamie scan the busy kitchen and identify the people most likely to stop any attempt to use the back stairs.

A tuxedo-clad waitress with long dark hair took a tray from one of the chefs. The woman tossed back her head in a familiar gesture and Jamie felt as if she'd been sucker punched. Her heart missed a beat. The woman swept the room with a cool gaze and left, heading toward the family room.

"What now?" Harrison demanded.

Jamie checked her impulse to dart after the figure as her adrenaline kicked into high gear. "That was Kirsten."

"Who?"

"One of your kidnappers."

Stunned, he stared at her. "I thought they both died in the fire."

"So did I."

"Did she see you?"

"I'm not sure."

"Let's go find her and find out what she had against that old farmhouse."

Jamie laid a restraining hand on his arm. "As much as I'd like to pull her aside and beat the snot out of her, I think we should leave right now."

"I pick option number one."

Her instincts were screaming. Something was going down here tonight. "Causing a scene is a bad idea. And without a bit of divine intervention, getting up those stairs doesn't look like an option, so unless you want to go outside in *that* and see if there's a way up from the deck, let's find a side door and live to fight another day."

That was the storm that had gathered force once more. The noisy flash and crash displays outside carried over the din of the party. The lights flickered once and abruptly went out.

People gasped. Someone actually shrieked. There was a crash and clatter from the kitchen. Jamie gripped his hand tightly. She'd been looking toward the back stairs when the lights went out. They had a clear path so she seized it.

There was a titter of laughter as voices were raised all around the crowded rooms. "I dropped the whole tray," someone nearby was exclaiming. "I need light over here!"

"Steps," she whispered, feeling for the bottom one.

"You really *are* good," Harrison murmured in her ear, following closely. "Divine intervention no less."

"I love a well-timed coincidence, but I'm not sure that's what this is. Quiet."

The darkness was absolute. Jamie knew there had to be at least one security person stationed upstairs, but there had been no time to debate their options. She'd chosen the path of least resistance. She hoped it wouldn't prove to be a fatal mistake.

The sounds from downstairs were audible but muted as she reached the top and began moving along the wall. Harrison's warm hand in hers and his presence close enough to kiss gave her added confidence. When she came to a door frame she stopped.

The handle opened easily under her hand and she guided them inside, closing the door behind them.

"Now what?" Harrison whispered in her ear.

The lights winked on without fanfare, flickered twice and went out again. The brief glimpse had allowed her to see that they were in a sitting room, most likely part of the master suite.

"I don't suppose you have a pocket flash?" she whispered back.

He leaned his head into hers until they touched. "In my suitcase in the trunk of your car. Want me to run outside and fetch it?"

"Hang on to that sense of humor. If we get caught up here, you're going to need it."

"If we get caught up here we tell them we were looking for a bed and some privacy."

She drew in an audible breath. "Like I said, hang on to that sense of humor."

"I can be quite convincing."

She couldn't believe his innuendo scored a direct hit. The murmur of voices froze any reply she might have summoned. A shaft of light suddenly illuminated the bottom of an ill-fitting door to their left. The hum of masculine voices faded away. The light remained.

Harrison brushed past her, heading in that direction. Her shin connected painfully with an invisible low table as she attempted to follow. His arms reached out to steady her before she stumbled, and she came up against his hard chest.

"Quiet," he murmured against her ear.

Outside, the storm rumbled agreement.

Releasing her, he continued on to the door.

Before she could stop him, he turned the handle. An older man sat on the edge of a huge bed putting on a pair of dark socks. A large, heavy-duty flashlight sat on the table at his side. He raised his head and looked right at them.

Jamie nearly gasped. Iris hadn't lied. Death waited in the shadows of this room as if growing impatient. Illness had ravaged what her memory told her had once been a robust, good-looking, powerful man. Fierce, dark eyes—mirrors of Harrison's—still held sharp intelligence.

Father and son stared at each other for the first time.

"So you came." Victor DiMarko's voice still carried power. "All the ghouls are gathering to pick over the bones."

"Should be an interesting show," Harrison told him levelly.

Victor DiMarko's surprising bark of laughter ended in a wracking coughing spree. Harrison didn't move. His father finally wiped at his mouth and then his eyes with a large linen hand-kerchief. The eyes turned to her.

"Tony's girl, Jamie, right?"

Startled as much by being addressed as the recognition, Jamie answered automatically. "Yes, sir."

"Odd combination. Planning to shoot me with that gun?"

She hadn't realized she'd drawn it from her bag. She lowered her hand quickly. "Do I need to?"

"I might consider it a kindness. Cancer's an ugly, mean bitch of a disease. Now, what would the two of you be doing here together?"

"We were invited," Harrison told him.

"Several times, as I recall," he agreed, "but you always said no."

"And I would have this time if it could have been avoided."

Victor DiMarko's rueful smile held no humor. "That means you need something from me at long last."

"Answers."

"Funny. I would have expected your mother to give you an earful of those years ago."

Harrison's voice hardened. "Let's leave my mother out of this. You were content to do so most of her life."

Even as she tensed, Jamie marveled at his calm.

"Did you arrange to have me kidnapped last night?"

The temperature in the room dropped ten degrees. Victor DiMarko straightened with remembered authority. In the deep shadows of the room it was hard to read his expressions.

"Again?" He sounded annoyed. "You seem to be making a habit of that. Looks like you didn't need my help getting free this time, either."

Jamie interrupted. "Can we postpone the family reunion? We need to find a safer location."

"You're safe here, girl."

"I don't think so, and don't call me *girl*." Her mind marveled at her daring stupidity as those piercing dark eyes fixed on her. It was all she could do not to squirm.

The lights winked back on. This time, they stayed on.

The bedroom door opened a beat later. The man standing there appeared shocked, but he took one look at the gun in her hand and reached inside his tuxedo.

"No, Frank."

Frank stopped moving. "Mr. DiMarko?"

"They were invited. Jamie, put your gun away. I'd prefer you don't shoot him. It's okay, Frank. They're my guests."

"That may be, sir, but Rolly isn't answering the radio. You need to move to the safe room now."

"Very well. They're with me." Victor's tone brooked no argument. He finished pulling on his sock, slid his feet into the loafers beside the bed and stood.

Frank closed the bedroom door and pressed the lock.

Harrison shook his head. "That wouldn't hold a three-year-old for more than a second."

"Long enough," Frank assured him.

"Harrison? Jamie? If you'll come with me we can finish this discussion in relative quiet."

Taking a .38 from the nightstand, he lifted the flashlight and moved toward his son. Harrison didn't budge until the other man strode right up to him. For a second Jamie thought he wouldn't step aside even then. It was obvious Victor wasn't going to alter his course. She held her breath until Harrison gave his father a hard look and finally stepped back.

The male posturing annoyed her, but given the circumstances, she supposed she should have been prepared for a dominance challenge.

Victor walked around the bed to where Frank was opening the door on the other side. A closet the size of a small bedroom was revealed. One corner held an organized set of shelves. Frank did something she couldn't see and the shelves pulled out to reveal a reinforced door. Beyond that was a bigger room with a bank of monitors, computer equipment, a gun rack, an overstuffed settee and two matching chairs.

"You're kidding," she muttered.

"It's a vault," Victor told them proudly, stepping inside.

"How's it hold up to plastique explosives?" she demanded.

"Someone tried to blow us up once already today," Harrison explained.

His father's jaw set. "Frank will see to it that that doesn't happen."

Jamie shook her head. "I think I'll take my chances out here."

Harrison touched her back lightly. "Jamie?"

"I don't like small places with no exits."

Frank spoke over her. "I just got a call that Mrs. DiMarko is looking for these two."

Victor narrowed his gaze. "Let her look." He spaced out the words. "These *guests* have my protection. You will not report their presence to anyone."

"Yes, *sir.*"

"Get inside, Jamie, so he can close the door." To Frank he added, "Check everyone's locations downstairs. If there is a threat of some sort, neutralize it. And let me know when I need to go down for that cake business. Otherwise, I don't want to be disturbed by anyone."

"Yes, sir."

Harrison prodded her forward and Jamie reluctantly entered. The entrance swung shut with a decisive sound and all outside noises faded.

"Ex-military?" Harrison asked his father.

"Dishonorably discharged," he agreed wryly.

"Naturally."

DiMarko set the flashlight down on a small table beside the chair without turning it off. He waited with the arrogance of command Jamie remembered so clearly. Harrison had inherited more than his father's dark eyes.

"You could turn it off," he suggested.

"I dislike the dark. I'll be seeing enough of it shortly." Victor DiMarko continued to stand by one of the chairs.

Belatedly, Jamie realized he was waiting for her to sit first. While unnerved, she wasn't fooled by his old-world manners. His weapon had disappeared, but this seemingly frail old man had built his fortune with little regard for others. If he decided the two of them needed to disappear, they'd need true divine intervention to see tomorrow. They were in the perfect spot to be shot with no one the wiser. It was a sobering thought.

Jamie perched on the edge of the couch. DiMarko sat with a small wince. To Jamie's surprise, instead of taking the other chair, Harrison sat beside her. A silent statement of solidarity? His welcome presence was reassuring.

"So, who kidnapped you this time?" Victor demanded.

"Me," she surprised herself by answering.

Those piercing dark eyes fixed on her. It was all she could do not to squirm.

"Why?"

She lifted her chin to meet his gaze. It would not do to quail before this man. "Tony asked me to."

His eyes narrowed. One large hand reached out toward a telephone on the table beside his chair.

"Tony's dead," she added.

The hand stilled. Slowly he withdrew his hand to grip the armrest with bony fingers. "How?"

Jamie drew on the rage she'd been keeping in check since she'd first walked into their house that morning. "He and Carolyn were executed. One shot to the back of the head."

A tic under his left eye was the only outward emotion he showed, but his stare was unnerving.

"We found them inside their house shortly after dawn."

And once again without warning, grief suddenly threatened to overwhelm her. Her voice actually cracked. Harrison laid a hand on her arm and squeezed gently.

"You thought I had them killed," DiMarko stated sadly.

"It was a possibility," Harrison agreed.

She fought for control. "Tony told me Harrison's kidnapping was a favor for a friend."

DiMarko nodded slowly. "So you assumed I was the friend."

"I didn't know who Harrison was at the time, but it seemed probable. I'm not sure Tony knew who he was, either."

"He knew." DiMarko looked to Harrison. "I had nothing to do with this. While I considered having you brought to me several times, I always rejected the idea. I wanted it to be your decision. It should have been." His gaze returned to Jamie. "Tony and Carolyn worked for me for many years. I considered them friends. Family. By extension, so are you. I will find out who did this."

"You already know," Harrison stated.

"Not conclusively, no. But I will. Tell me exactly what happened."

Jamie met Harrison's gaze. He inclined his head, so she related the events of the past twenty-four hours. Her deep unease grew in proportion to the older man's silence. She'd never seen a person sit so still. If he blinked, she didn't notice, but once she finished he sighed again.

"I did not ask Tony to arrange this kidnapping. The truth is I had made arrangements to attend your wedding, Harrison."

Harrison jolted.

"I may not have been a father to you while you were growing up, but I have never forgotten that I have three sons. I did my best to keep that fact a closely held secret over the years for your protection. Unfortunately, secrets rarely stay that way. I have been having problems lately with an ambitious rival. It is regrettable that this person holds me responsible for the death of his youngest son. I was not to blame in this instance, but he is forcing me into a position I dislike. You are *my* youngest son, Harrison. I have reason to believe my rival recently learned of your existence. As my other children are well protected, I was concerned for your safety so I arranged extra security for your wedding."

"The sniper on the roof was yours?" Jamie asked.

"No. I'm afraid for once the police did me a good turn by arresting the man. The sniper was there to kill one or both of us. Fortunately, someone—you?—informed the police in time and when we drove up and saw all the activity, Frank insisted the church was too risky so we left. I was disturbed, thinking your wedding had been interrupted."

"Was Wayne Drake one of your people?" Harrison asked.

Victor frowned. "No, as far as I know, Drake was a small-time independent."

"Then who tried to kill Zoe? Your rival?"

"Highly unlikely. I believe the police considered Drake a suspect in a major gem theft. Their feeling seems to be that his death was a result of a falling-out among thieves."

"What do you believe?"

"I hadn't given Drake more than a passing thought and only that much because of his connection to your fiancée. I must ask, is she pregnant with your baby or Drake's?"

He held up a hand as Harrison tensed. "I realize it's none of my business, but I am dying, Harrison. I'd very much like to know if she carries my first grandchild."

Harrison didn't move for an endless second. Then he looked at Jamie. "No, she doesn't."

She had no idea why he'd directed his answer to her, but her heart beat faster all the same. That the baby wasn't his shouldn't matter, but it did.

Victor eyed them closely. "I see."

Harrison regarded his father with a tight look. "I don't know what you think you see, but I believe someone in this house ordered the murder of Jamie's foster parents and tried to kill Jamie and me."

"Yes. I appreciate that you didn't go to the police with this. The situation with my rival will be resolved shortly and I will deal with the rest."

Harrison glared at his father. "Are you saying your rival killed Tony and Ceecee?"

"Ceecee. Do you know, your mother was the only one who ever called her that?"

There was a wistfulness in his gaze and in his voice for just a second. Jamie wondered if Harrison's mother hadn't meant more to Victor than Harrison believed.

"I'm saying I will discover who killed Tony and Carolyn and will take appropriate measures."

As Harrison started to bristle, the vault door opened and Frank stuck his head inside. "The house is secure, Mr. DiMarko. Mrs. DiMarko is still looking for these two."

Victor DiMarko straightened in authority. "You have your orders."

"Yes, sir."

"Find one of the serving women named Kirsten. Bring her here."

"Yes, sir."

No one moved as he left, closing the heavy vault door behind him.

"I take care of my own," Victor stated into the silence. "Did you know that when you were kidnapped as a boy, your mother called me asking for help? It was the only time she ever asked me for anything."

"And you said no."

His tone sharpened. "Don't be naive, Harrison. You're a businessman, too. I might demand a ransom, but I would never pay one any more than you would. Paying it would have ensured your death. I told her as much and she hung up on me. That didn't mean I wasn't prepared to help. You escaped on your own before my people arrived."

There was pride in his voice and on his worn features.

"We did come for you. The men who took you were punished."

"You killed them."

He didn't flinch. "The threat was neutralized. I made it a point to see to it that you and your mother were never troubled again. Your mother rejected all my requests to meet you after that, and against my better judgment, I respected her wishes. I've come to regret that mistake. Still, she did an excellent job raising you. You've created quite an empire on your own."

"We aren't in the same line of work."

He smiled without humor. "Don't be so sure. I have many legitimate avenues now."

Once again the door opened. Frank stood there looking troubled. "Mr. DiMarko, the woman left a short while ago. Angie says she complained of feeling sick."

"Have someone find her. Quietly."

"Yes, sir."

He had started to close the door when a slim hand pushed it open. "Daddy, Mother wants— oh."

There was no warmth in Fay's gaze as she took in the scene. Her pencil-thin navy gown displayed a generous amount of cleavage and hugged every slim curve, leaving little of her shape to the imagination. "Am I interrupting?"

"It's fine, princess," her father assured her. "Are we ready for the cake cutting?"

"Yes. Mother wants to know if you feel up to attending."

"Tell her I'll be right there. Better yet, I'll go down with you."

DiMarko stood. Harrison rose as well, so Jamie joined them.

"Harrison, have you met your sister, Fay?"

"Yes, this afternoon."

"Good. I'd like you to wait here while I get this business over with. There's more we need to discuss."

"I don't think so."

"Please."

Fay sucked in a breath. Obviously, *please* was not a word she was used to hearing from her father.

"Will we be able to leave when we're done?" Harrison asked without flinching at the steel gaze his father leveled at him.

"My word on that. You may wish to move

into the sitting room while you wait as Jamie is uncomfortable in here. Frank will show you. There's a bar. Feel free to help yourselves. If you want anything else, Frank will get it for you. This won't take long."

The fleeting look of fury in Fay's eyes raised every hair on Jamie's arms. Her expression immediately changed to one of passive adoration as she took her father's arm and led him from the room.

Jamie turned to Harrison. "Did you see—?"

"Always good to know we're making friends everywhere we go," he agreed. He smiled at Frank, who watched them intently. Frank didn't smile back.

"This way."

As relieved as she was to leave the vault, Jamie gazed around at the sitting room through which they'd originally entered. Designed with comfort it mind, it still felt entirely too much like a trap.

"I'll be in the hall," Frank announced.

The minute he closed the door, she moved to the sliding glass door across the room. "We've overstayed our welcome."

"I think you're right."

Her eyes roved the door. "It's wired to an alarm system."

"No surprise there. Victor's big on security."

"I can't see if there's a way down from here even if we ignore the alarm."

"Then let's see if Frank will let us leave."

He opened the door to the hall. Frank straightened from his position against the opposite wall. "Help you?"

"We've decided to go down and have some cake."

"I'll have some brought up for you. Mr. DiMarko wants you to wait here."

"Okay. Ask them to bring a pot of black coffee as well." Harrison stepped back inside and closed the door. "I don't suppose you can summon another one of your divine interventions."

"Fresh out." She eyed the bed in the room

beyond and cocked her head. "Think you can fit under there?"

"You want me to hide under the bed? We have guns, remember?"

"So do they. Guns are messy. Let's make them a last resort."

Harrison eyed the bed. "Jamie, I'm too tired for games. I'd rather be on top of the bed with you than under it. Let's just go."

She should have known. Harrison was used to giving orders, not following them. He opened the door to the hall and gave her a none too gentle nudge. "Keep walking."

Voices wafted up from downstairs, singing the traditional birthday song. Frank pounded up behind them. "Wait!"

Harrison didn't slow. "Tell Victor we had to leave, but I'll call him."

He whirled to face Frank before the man could grab his arm. "He won't be happy if you shoot us and neither will his guests. Blood doesn't go with cake and ice cream. We aren't going to make a scene and I advise you not to do the same without checking."

"The police are looking for Harrison and the people who kidnapped him," Jamie put in. "It wouldn't be a good thing for them to find him being held here against his will."

Frank hesitated. Harrison snagged Jamie's arm and started walking again. A second guard appeared at the top of the stairs. He watched, but didn't try to stop them when they reached his position. They didn't look back to see Frank's reaction.

"Did you forget we still have the problem of locating the car?" she asked softly as they started down the stairs.

Harrison realized he had forgotten. "We could leave it and walk."

"I prefer plan B."

"Which is?"

Jamie shrugged. "No idea, but it won't require a long hike in the rain."

"Afraid you'll melt?"

"That was the evil witch. I'm the good one, remember?"

He smiled as they reached the bottom of the stairs, where a third tuxedo-clad muscleman eyed them darkly. Applause came from the rear of the house. Harrison nodded to the guard and strode to the front door.

The young man who'd taken their car when they arrived jumped forward, hastily pinching out a pungent cigarette that he shoved into his jacket pocket.

"Black, four-door sedan—"

"Yes, sir, I remember. I'll be right back," he promised, scampering away.

Harrison raised his eyebrows. "Should we worry that he remembers us?"

"More than likely it was the only car he parked tonight that sells in a price range *he* could afford."

"I guess that would make us memorable. No one's started shooting yet."

Her hand flicked open the snap on her purse.

"We're still on the grounds. It's dark and private and raining. Plus, let's not forget Kirsten is missing."

"You inspire such confidence." Fatigue was making him sloppy. He'd forgotten all about Kirsten. Good thing Jamie was still thinking straight.

"If they're going to stop us, it will be at the gate," she cautioned.

"Think positive."

There was no humor in the gaze she turned on him. "I'm positive that's where they'll try to stop us."

He tipped the youth who brought the car around, a little surprised no one had come out and asked them to step back inside.

Jamie slipped behind the wheel. The moment he was inside she started the car down the drive. As Harrison fastened his seat belt he realized she held her gun in one hand. "I thought that was a last resort."

"So's the gate."

It was almost anticlimactic when the guard merely waved them through the open gate.

"Problem solved."

"Think so?" Jamie shook her head. "We need to dump this car."

"What is it with you and cars?"

"Remember what I told you about letting your drink out of sight? This car has been out of our sight a long time. Victor likes technology and Kirsten likes to play with plastique explosives."

She pulled over on a grassy strip in front of another private estate two blocks over. "Grab the flashlight from the glove compartment and get out of the car."

She was already out. Harrison located a high-beam flashlight and joined her in the rain where she had the hood up, peering inside at the jumbled mess of machinery.

"Know anything about engines?" he asked.

"They make the car go," she replied.

His lips curved. "How did you know there'd be a flashlight in the glove compartment?"

"It's Tony's car."

Apparently that explained everything.

"Stand over there and let me do my job, Harrison."

"Do you really think Kirsten placed a bomb on the car?"

"Or a tracer. Call me paranoid."

"Not anymore."

She closed the hood and began covering every inch of the sedan. He almost said something when she got down on the wet ground and slowly shone the flashlight over the undercarriage.

"No explosives?" he asked when she finished.

"None I could find, but there's a homing device attached to the rear bumper."

"Did you remove it?"

She brushed ineffectively at the mud on her thoroughly wet pants. The entire outfit was so wet it was plastered to her skin. He really liked that outfit.

"No point. It probably isn't the only one."

A passing small car slowed, then pulled in front of them and stopped.

Chapter Eight

"Get down!" Jamie ordered. She had her revolver in her hand again by the time the driver's door opened. Harrison crouched beside her, fumbling for the gun he'd tucked into his back waistband.

An umbrella appeared. Liz Sylor stepped from the car.

"Hey, are you okay? Do you need some help?"

Jamie came out of her crouch, weapon still in hand, hidden by the wet folds of her slacks. "The transmission went."

"Oh. Do you want a lift somewhere?"

"We're pretty wet."

"I'll say. I've got a blanket in the trunk."

Jamie looked to Harrison. He shrugged to indicate it was her call.

"So do I," she agreed slowly. "I'll get it from the trunk."

Liz waited as they stepped around to the rear of the car.

"Divine intervention again?" he whispered.

"We'll find out."

He raised his eyebrows and grabbed his suitcase while she pulled a blanket from the depths of the trunk.

"Stay alert," she cautioned.

Jamie insisted on riding in the backseat to minimize the mess inside the car. Liz agreed and Harrison got a clear view of her face in the overhead light. Her mascara had run, leaving streaks over red and puffy-looking eyes. "Are you all right, Liz?"

She wouldn't meet his gaze. "I'm fine. Where to?"

"The nearest metro station would be great," Jamie answered. "We'll send a mechanic out in the morning. The car will need to be towed, but it should be okay where it is for now."

"I'd be happy to drive you home."

"We aren't going home," Harrison told her, "but thanks for stopping. Did Lyle hurt you?"

She met his gaze in the rearview mirror. "No. He left me alone after you scared him off, but his sister and his mother made it pretty clear they aren't ever going to approve of me. I know we can't pick our family—"

"Sure you can," Jamie interjected. "You just have to be willing to walk away from what you know and start fresh."

And that, he thought, said a lot about Jamie's past.

"I don't think Gordon can do that." Liz's voice thickened.

"If he loves you enough, anything is possible," Jamie told her. "And if he doesn't, it's better you find out now rather than later."

"I know you're right." She sniffed. "It just hurts, you know?"

This was the sort of conversation a man was better off staying out of, he decided. He focused on the road as they turned onto a busy thoroughfare. A pair of headlights growing rapidly in the side mirror caught his attention. Far too rapidly.

"Jamie." Harrison pointed to the mirror. There was no question. The car was racing up behind them.

"Is something wrong?" Liz asked.

Jamie swore, but it was too late, the car was already on top of them.

"What is that crazy fool doing?" Liz demanded.

"Get down," Jamie ordered Harrison as the oncoming car swerved around them, then cut back in front of them, braking hard.

Amazingly, Liz brought her car to a stop without hydroplaning on the slick road. She didn't even hit the other vehicle.

"Get out!" Jamie had the back door open and was tugging on his arm.

"What's going on?" Liz asked fearfully as Harrison added to Jamie's order.

"Get down, Liz!" Sliding out of the car, he crouched with Jamie as a lone figure sprang from the other vehicle and started toward them.

Jamie held her gun pointed at the indistinct, suit-clad figure. Either he never saw them or he didn't care. He ran straight to the driver's door and flung it open.

"Liz!" In the headlights of a passing car, Gordon's features were distraught. "Why did you leave?"

Jamie muttered something under her breath and relaxed. The gun disappeared. Harrison stood.

Liz burst into tears. "It's over, Gordon. Your family is never going to allow us to marry."

"I don't give a damn about my family."

"Yes, you do. They'll never accept me."

"I told you I don't care."

"They're your family," she wailed.

"I want *you* to be my family. I love you."

"So much for a quick getaway." Jamie sighed.

Gordon seemed to see them for the first time.

He let go of Liz and stood to face them. "What are *you* doing here?"

"We *were* getting a lift to the metro station. You're blocking traffic." A car honked sharply as the driver pulled around them. "We need to get out of the road."

"Pull in over there," Gordon ordered, indicating a small shopping plaza. "If you leave, I'll just follow," he told Liz.

"We should have risked the bomb," Jamie muttered.

Harrison nodded. "Should we see if we can call a cab?"

"Their car broke down," Liz was saying. "I wasn't running from you."

"Of course you were. I told you to let me handle things."

"You weren't doing a very good job of it," Harrison couldn't resist saying.

"Get in the car, Harrison," Jamie urged.

"What do you mean?" Gordon demanded.

"I had to rescue her from Lyle. Apparently,

after that, your mother and sister had a go at her."

His brother's expression turned thunderous. "Did one of them hurt you?" he demanded of Liz.

"Of course not. I'm not afraid of your family."

"You should be," Harrison told her.

Furious, Gordon glared at him. "You stay out of this!"

Jamie stepped between them. "Liz, park the car. We need to get out of the street before a helpful police officer comes along and arrests all of us for impeding the flow of traffic."

"Over there," Gordon ordered, storming back to his sports car.

They piled back into the car and Liz followed Gordon into the parking lot. He was out of his car and sprinting for theirs before Liz could turn off the ignition. Gordon opened the passenger door and slid inside. Jamie had her hand in her purse once more.

Harrison leaned forward, ignoring his brother's scowl. "Gordon, you probably don't want any advice from me, but if you're serious about marrying the girl, catch the red-eye to Vegas, find a chapel and be done with it. Then take her on an extended honeymoon and find a job as far from Virginia and your family as you can. Liz says you're a decent architect. Go be an architect. I know a few people. I might be able to help you, if you want."

"What's in it for you?"

"For one thing it might get us home sooner." Jamie's lips twitched.

Despite his scowl, some of Gordon's belligerence lessened. "Feel free to leave anytime. Liz and I need to talk."

"I promised them a ride home."

Gordon tossed his keys over the seat to Harrison, who caught them out of the air. "Take my car."

"And get stopped for grand theft auto?" Harrison tossed them back. "No, thanks."

"I'm giving you the damn car."

"Generous, but we'll pass."

"You could take mine," Liz offered.

Gordon spun toward her. "Does that mean you'll come with me?"

"Not back to your parents' house."

"No. We'll go to Mike's apartment. I still have the key. Unless… Would you be willing to do what he said?"

"You mean fly to Vegas?"

"Why not? He's right, once we're married, what can anyone do?"

Harrison exchanged a quick glance with Jamie. "You *are* talking about *your* family, right?"

Gordon shot Harrison a dark glare. "They're your family, too."

"Not so much."

Jamie intervened. "The jury's out on you, Gordon, but I like Liz and I have to agree with Harrison. I wouldn't trust the rest of your family any further than I could throw a rhinoceros. Lyle threatened Liz once tonight."

His features darkened. "I'll deal with Lyle."

"How does Victor feel about your union?" Harrison asked.

"We haven't discussed it. My father and I don't talk much. I'm a disappointment to him."

"Good for you."

That seemed to surprise him. "None of us measure up to you."

"Because he's his own person," Jamie told him. "His success isn't measured on the coattails of his father."

Startled, Harrison stared at her.

"It's true," Jamie assured him. "You never asked him for anything, you wouldn't even see him when he wanted you to. You stood up to him, even tonight."

"Tonight?" Gordon asked.

"Long story," Harrison told his brother, not looking away from Jamie.

"Victor uses intimidation, coercion, bribery, whatever it takes to get what he wants. You made it through guts and hard work." She turned her gaze to Gordon. "That's what your father respects. He has everything he's ever wanted except respectability. Now that he's dying, I think he regrets that."

"Your father is dying?" Liz asked Gordon, looking shocked.

"He has terminal cancer. It's supposed to be a family secret."

Harrison shrugged. "I was serious about my offer to help you."

"Again, why?"

"Primarily because I need to go to bed at some point tonight and this seems like the quickest way to get rid of both of you."

"Harrison's a sucker for a happy ending," Jamie put in.

"I will get you for that."

"You can try," she told him. "I'm tired, too."

"Do you really want to go to Vegas and elope?" Liz asked.

Gordon's gaze said it all. "Yes."

Her smile lit her face. "Then let's go."

"You mean it? Don't you want the fancy wedding with the dress and all the trimmings?"

"I've only ever wanted you."

Jamie rolled her eyes. Harrison winked at her.

"You've got me."

"I'm starting to feel like a voyeur here," Jamie whispered.

Harrison grinned and she smiled back.

"Why don't you come with us?" Liz asked abruptly. "We could have a double wedding."

"We aren't a couple," Jamie squeaked. "I'm his bodyguard. Harrison already has a fiancée."

"Oh. I thought…I mean, you two seemed so right together. That is, I didn't mean…"

Jamie's abrupt dismissal of them as a couple rankled, though it shouldn't have. Harrison *was* engaged until he talked to Zoe. He had no right to feel annoyed. But he was.

"No harm done," he assured Liz.

"We should go, Liz."

"So should we," Harrison agreed. "We'll call a cab."

"Take my car," Gordon demanded. "I'm damn sure not going to leave it sitting in an airport parking lot to be stolen. We'll take Liz's car."

Harrison measured his brother. Finally he nodded. "All right."

"Thank you," Liz told them. "Both of you. I'm glad Gordon has one family member he can count on."

Harrison and Gordon exchanged wry looks. "I like Liz. Take care of her," Harrison said.

"I intend to."

Jamie waited while Harrison took his suitcase from the trunk and followed him to what proved to be a deep blue Porsche.

Stowing the suitcase in the small trunk, Harrison tipped his head. "You want to drive or shall I?"

"Funny man." She moved around to the driver's side.

"Not going to check it for bombs first?" he asked.

Jamie hesitated for a brief second. "Let's live dangerously."

Harrison laughed out loud. As they climbed inside, Gordon ran over to them. Harrison opened the door.

"Mind giving me a number where I can reach you?"

"Worried about your car already?"

His gaze darkened. "I thought you were serious about the job."

"I am." Harrison dug for his wallet and pulled out a card. "Got a pen?"

"In the glove compartment."

"What's your cell phone number, Jamie?"

She gave it to him reluctantly and he wrote it down along with two other numbers. "This is my direct line at work. The other number belongs to Arthur Van Wheeler. He's a close friend. If you can't reach me, try him."

"Okay." He hesitated. "Thanks."

"I hope it all works out for you." And strangely enough, he meant the words. His brother held his gaze.

"Me, too."

"And, Gordon?" His brother paused. "Happy birthday."

Gordon gave him a two-finger salute and ran back toward Liz's car. Jamie had a feeling the two of them might actually become friends one day.

"Think they'll make it?" she asked.

"The original Romeo and Juliet didn't fare so well."

"There is that."

They drove straight back to the motel without further incident despite the fretful watch Jamie kept on the headlights behind them.

"I'll take the couch," he offered, feeling the crushing weight of exhaustion sapping what little energy he had left. "You can take the bed."

"We'll both take the bed."

He raised his eyebrows, ignoring the way his tired body wanted to leap to conclusions.

"I trust you."

"Now who's being naive?" he asked with a smile to show her he was teasing.

"You're engaged to be married. I assume you don't want me to emasculate you."

"Ouch. You'd do it, too."

"Believe it. I'm going to get out of these wet clothes."

"Let me grab a towel from the bathroom first."

The scene was pleasingly domestic. Harrison was surprised by how good he felt despite the drag of his eyelids. He wasn't surprised when he heard the shower start up a few minutes later. Jamie had, after all, lain in the mud and dirt at the side of the road.

Stripping off his wet clothing, he pulled out the running shorts and top he'd packed to take on his honeymoon. Sleeping in the nude wasn't an option tonight, even if she had already seen all of him there was to see.

It was too late to try calling Zoe or Artie again, but Zoe should be fine. She had Artie, Carter and Ramsey Incorporated watching over her. He had complete faith in all of them, especially Zoe.

Jamie was taking her time in the shower and he could barely keep his eyes open. Crossing to the bed, he lay down on top of the spread to wait for her and closed his eyes.

HARRISON AWOKE to a dark room and the sound of muffled sobbing. Without moving, he knew the other side of the huge bed was empty. The noise came from the living area.

The clock on the nightstand showed he'd been asleep less than an hour. Rolling from the bed, he zeroed in on the sound and found a huddled shape curled on the small couch clutching a pillow.

"Jamie."

He'd spoken softly, barely above a whisper, but her head jerked up as if he'd yelled.

"I didn't mean to wake you." Her voice was clogged with the tears she tried vainly to wipe from her cheeks.

He perched on the seat beside her. "Come 'ere."

The pillow fell to the floor as her body tensed with rejection. He gathered her into his arms anyhow. "It's okay. Cry it out. You're long overdue."

As if the words were a signal, the dam broke once again. "I loved them."

"I know."

She pressed her face against his chest, sobbing as if her heart had shattered. Maybe it had. Her grief made his own eyes well and he had to blink and swallow hard. Her wet hair smelled faintly of coconut and he stroked it softly, wanting to ease her pain somehow.

"I hadn't seen Ceecee since I was fourteen." His quiet words seemed right with the rhythm of her sobs. "I hadn't thought about her for a long time. But seeing her like that…" He had to clear his throat. "Her death was my last living connection to my mother and my past. Ceecee—Carolyn—" he corrected "—was sunshine and laughter in our world. She was my mother's best friend. And she didn't deserve to die like that."

He rocked Jamie gently in his arms, feeling

her shaking and was surprised to realize his own eyes brimmed with tears that ran unchecked down his cheeks as memories flooded him. It seemed important that he share them with her, a connection only she would understand.

"Ceecee used to come and visit us a lot when I was young." He let the memories wash over him. All of them good, and he'd nearly forgotten them. "The world was always brighter and more fun when she came. Not because she always brought gifts, or even because she never talked down to me or treated me like a nuisance. What I remember most is the sound of her laughter. She had such an incredible laugh."

Jamie's head bobbed in agreement.

"She brought so much joy to our lives. For fourteen years, she never once forgot my birthday. She'd send me what seemed like an amazing amount of money and tell me to buy myself something I really wanted. But I never did. I put the money in the bank and when I'd see her next she'd ask what I did with it and I'd tell her. She'd smile and hug me and tell me she loved me."

Jamie drew in a deep shuddery breath.

"I didn't know her husband. Didn't even know she was married. I only knew that when Ceecee came, it was like Christmas morning all over again, bright and shiny and exciting. I missed her terribly when she stopped coming."

Until now, he'd forgotten how much.

Jamie sniffed and lifted her head. Her muffled voice was thick and husky. "Why did she stop?"

"Because of my kidnapping." He heard the hard anger in his tone and strove to soften it. "We moved a lot after that because my mother never felt safe again. She wouldn't talk about it, but I think she was afraid someone would use Ceecee to get at me. Or maybe she was afraid someone would use Ceecee against her. I don't know. It's what I thought as a kid."

Jamie pulled back and gazed at him. His shoulders rose and fell. "The only thing I know for sure is that it was hard on both of us when her visits stopped. My mother missed her terribly even though I knew they stayed in touch with phone calls. But those always preceded another move. Nothing was ever the same after my kidnapping."

"It wasn't your fault," she managed.

"No, but I was fourteen and it felt like my fault at the time. Mom wouldn't talk about Ceecee after that, not even when I knew they'd been talking together."

The memory was still painful. His mother had never shut him out before.

"Mom used to tell me stories about the trouble the two of them got into as kids. Like the time they scratched her dad's car with a bike and tried to cover the mark with a can of green paint they found."

Jamie hiccupped and smiled. "Carolyn told me that story. I didn't know it was your mother, but I knew it was a friend she'd loved a lot."

Harrison nodded. "They stayed best friends all their lives. I know Ceecee was there for her when Mom's parents died when she was in college. She didn't have any other relatives that I ever knew about, so Ceecee was our only family. I can still hear her laugh. I wish I'd gone to the effort to find her after my mother passed away."

"Why didn't you?"

"While intellectually I knew it wasn't her fault, I still felt like she abandoned us. When Mom knew she was dying, they talked, but Ceecee never came. I kept thinking she would. Near the end, I even asked my mother if I should call and ask her to come. I was a grown man, but I really wanted Ceecee to be there. Mom wouldn't let me call her."

His mother's fierce tone had been so unlike her that he'd backed off and hadn't even gone looking for Ceecee's number after his mother died.

"Because she worked for Victor?" Jamie asked.

"Probably. I never knew about that, but now it seems reasonable that that's why Ceecee didn't try and get in touch with me. I think Mom asked her not to. She was still worried about me even though I was an adult. I missed her, Jamie. She shouldn't have died like that."

Jamie nodded, eyes brimming once more. His own eyes burned with unspilled tears and Jamie surprised him by laying her head on his shoulder. He held her for a long while before the aftermath of her sobs finally quieted. Both of them were too spent to move, but when his head nodded, bumping hers because he was more asleep than awake, he released her gently. "Let's go to bed. You have nothing to fear from me."

"I know." And she kissed him lightly on the cheek. "Thank you."

He nodded and stood, pulling her to her feet. Bending, he picked up the forgotten pillow and carried it to the bed for her.

"Uh, Jamie, don't take this wrong, but I need to take off this shirt. It's too wet to sleep in now."

She managed a weak smile and climbed into bed. "Come to bed, Harrison."

Slipping off the shirt, he dropped it on the

dresser and pulled back the covers, careful to stay on his edge of the bed. "Good night, Jamie."

"Harrison? Could you…just hold me for a while? I promise not to cry anymore."

He turned, unable to see her features in the dark room. "Cry all you want. Ceecee was worth any amount of tears."

"So was Tony."

"I'm glad. I'm glad she had him. And that you had both of them." He drew her against his bare chest, feeling the silent, heaving breaths that were the legacy of so many tears. Stroking her hair one last time, he kissed her on the forehead. "Sleep now. I've got you."

"Who has you?" Her voice was blurred with sleep.

"You do. Sleep."

Chapter Nine

Harrison awoke to find Jamie staring at him, her hand hovering in midair as if about to stroke his cheek. She lowered it instantly and started to roll away. He snagged her waist, preventing the move. "Good morning."

"Let me go."

He released her and she scooted off the bed, rushing into the bathroom. Stretching, he savored the faint scent of coconut on the pillow they had shared and the heady knowledge of what he'd glimpsed so clearly in her eyes for that one brief instant.

Yearning. Jamie had feelings for him beyond friendship, whether she wanted to admit it or not.

People called to one another outside. Car doors slammed. An engine started up. A maid's trolley rolled to a stop nearby and someone rapped on a door. Despite the heavy drapes covering the windows, blocking out light, it was obviously morning.

And Jamie wanted him.

She reminded him of the wary cat his mother had tamed once when he was young. It had taken months, but when they moved the next time, the cat came with them. It gradually came not only to accept them, but to seek out their companionship. It would sit beside his mother on the couch and purr as she stroked its fur.

Smiling, Harrison decided food probably wouldn't work as an incentive with Jamie, but he was pretty sure he could find another way to earn her trust. And that was something he wanted very much.

Like with his mother's cat, life had taught Jamie some harsh lessons. The military would have reinforced them because being tougher and stronger than anyone else meant survival. Gentle emotions, especially tears, were a sign of weakness.

Jamie hadn't fled to the bathroom because she was afraid. She'd fled because she was embarrassed that he'd seen her vulnerable. Right now she was in there fortifying her barriers. She didn't realize barriers were nothing new to Harrison. He had a number of them himself and he'd learned patience. He'd find the chinks and get past her walls eventually.

But first he needed to talk with Zoe. She'd understand. They were friends first and foremost. He'd never abandon her or her child, but he could no longer marry her. Given that he was pretty sure she'd been having second thoughts about their marriage, he suspected she would agree that it would have been a mistake.

Sliding out of bed, he dropped to the floor and began a series of push-ups in lieu of his morning run. The bathroom door opened when he was partway through.

"I'm going to go for a quick run," Jamie announced.

Harrison stopped and stood. "You like to run, too?" Reaching for his T-shirt, he smiled. "Let's go."

She avoided eye contact, frowning.

"Think I can't keep up?"

"I usually run four miles."

"Perfect, so do I. Let me use the bathroom and I'll be right with you. You might want to put the Do Not Disturb card out. I heard the maid out there a few minutes ago."

He thought she'd come up with another excuse, but when he came out of the bathroom a few minutes later she was doing stretches while she waited.

She surprised him again by not setting a hard pace to test him. Of course, the late August heat was already building, but they pounded along in companionable silence.

It wasn't until they reached the parking lot once more that she stopped abruptly, tugging on his arm. "Wait!"

"What's wrong?"

"I'm not sure." Jamie studied the scene.

So did he. "That Aston Martin wasn't there before. You don't think…?" They exchanged glances. "How?"

"They had a tracking device on his car."

Harrison grimaced. "You did say we should live dangerously."

She got the reference immediately. "Stupid of me. Let's go." Jamie turned and started back the way they'd come.

"Where are we going?"

"I'm thinking."

"Have you got your cell phone?" Harrison asked.

"Yes, why?"

"Do you have Victor's number?"

Jamie hesitated. "I'm not sure calling him is such a good idea."

"Letting our opponent call the shots is a sure way to come out on the losing end."

"Especially when the shots come from a gun," she agreed, and handed him the cell phone.

A woman answered. "I'm sorry, sir. Mr. DiMarko isn't available right now."

"All right, let me speak with his bodyguard, Frank. It's important."

If the woman was surprised by the request she didn't show her surprise. "One moment, Mr. Trent."

"Good thinking," Jamie whispered.

Time ticked past. "Maybe not. Can they trace us using this call?"

"The government could. I'm not sure about them, but it's taking too long. Hang up."

Frank's voice filled his ear. "Constantine."

Harrison hit Speakerphone. "It's Trent. I told you we'd call."

"Mr. DiMarko said to put you through, but he's meeting with his lawyer right now. Should I interrupt?"

"That depends. Did he send someone after us?"

There was a beat of silence. "No. You got trouble?"

"Maybe. Who in the family drives a silver Aston Martin?"

"Mrs. DiMarko." Frank sounded surprised.

"Is she there?"

The hesitation was thoughtful. "No, she left the house over an hour ago."

"Alone?"

"Yeah. Arturo is ticked. Look, Mr. DiMarko said I was to help if you needed help. I'll go interrupt."

"Don't bother, Frank. Did you find Kirsten?"

"Parsons? She didn't go home last night. Her roommate hasn't seen her." He sounded annoyed.

"Where does she live?"

"She's got a place in the District near the Maryland line." He recited the address. "I can meet you there in twenty or thirty minutes if you want."

"If she isn't there, there's not much point." Kirsten Parsons wouldn't be returning to her place any time soon if she had the sense of a housefly. "I need to go see what Mrs. DiMarko wants."

Concern filled Frank's voice. "Mr. DiMarko won't like it."

"I don't, either, but tell Victor I'll call him back and let him know how the discussion went." Harrison disconnected without waiting for a response.

Jamie frowned. "You aren't serious."

"If she's alone..."

"And if she isn't?"

"You wait outside and go for help."

"As if."

He grinned. "I assume you're armed."

She gave him a scornful look. He grinned unrepentantly. "Would you miss me if I got killed?"

"You've no idea how much," she told him mock sweetly. "I'd have to spend weeks answering questions and filling out paperwork."

"I knew you'd come to value me eventually."

He touched her cheek lightly and told her seriously, "I trust you to cover my back, Jamie. Let's go see what the evil stepmother wants."

Scowling, she gave him a none-too-gentle shove. "I'm going in first."

"While I appreciate the sacrifice, it looks like that won't be necessary."

The door to their unit opened. Iris DiMarko stepped outside and peered around the parking lot with obvious impatience. It took only a second before her gaze fastened on them. The look turned bitter as they approached.

"Where's Gordon?" she asked.

"Good morning, Iris. What an unexpected surprise."

She looked as if she'd been up all night. Her usually impeccable hair was mussed, her makeup nonexistent and lines of distress marred her features. "Where is he? That's his car."

"It is, yes. He lent it to us last night."

Her features crumpled without warning. Tears rolled down her cheeks. She brushed them away with short, choppy gestures. Harrison turned her around and led her back inside the motel room, exchanging a long look with Jamie over her head.

By the time she settled on the couch, she had herself back under control. She stopped in the act of reaching inside a large handbag when Jamie leveled a gun at her head.

"I guess I deserve that. I just want some tissues."

She withdrew a small package with exaggerated care, pulled several free and dabbed at her eyes. "He left with that girl, didn't he?"

"Her name is Liz," Jamie reminded her, lowering the gun but keeping it visible in her hand.

Iris snapped, "I know her name. Do you know who her father is?"

"The district attorney," Harrison replied. "She told us."

"Did she also tell you that her father has been trying to indict *your* father on any charge he could find for the past three years?"

"Why does that surprise you? Victor made his living flouting the law."

"He's your father!"

"Genetically speaking, but he's never been a father to me, Iris, and you know it."

Her lips compressed in a tight line. "You'd let him go to jail?"

"You're getting ahead of yourself here."

"Gordon's besotted with that stupid girl." She balled up the tissue angrily.

"Do you think her parents are any happier than you are?"

The question obviously hadn't occurred to her. Her mouth went slack.

"You should be happy. Your son is lucky enough to be marrying a woman who truly loves him." He looked at Jamie. "Some people never find the right fit. Or find it too late."

Iris snorted. "Don't be a fool. Love is just sex in disguise."

Again, he glanced at Jamie. "Not always." He shook his head at Iris. "What are you worried about? Does Gordon have something to fear from the D.A.'s office? I was told he's an architect."

Iris dismissed that subject with a swipe of her hand and leaned forward intently. "Right this minute Victor is with his lawyer redoing his will. Gordon deserves to be part of our organization. Victor will cut him out completely if he marries that girl."

He wondered if she realized how telling that comment was.

"Did you ever ask Gordon what he wanted?" Jamie asked.

Harrison jumped in to head off the gleam of sudden anger. "Iris, if you continue to press him you'll lose your son one way or another. He's an adult. Let him make his own choices."

"This is your fault!" She spat the words at him, her pale face mottled with anger. "I gave Victor three strong children and all he can talk about is his little bastard. I will not stand by and see my children cut out of their inheritance." She started to reach into her purse.

"Move one more finger and I'll blow it off."

Jamie's voice could have sliced steel. Her gun was once more leveled on the woman. Harrison didn't doubt for a moment that she'd pull the trigger. Apparently, Iris believed it as well. She stilled instantly.

Harrison knew one wrong word would send this supercharged moment spiraling out of control. "Iris, I want no part of Victor's organization. Or anything else of his for that matter."

"Bastard."

He flinched at the venom in her voice. Her former calm facade was in tatters. Harrison couldn't help feeling a twinge of sympathy for her. "I'm not responsible for that, either."

She stood up, body trembling, her face suffused with rage. Jamie held the gun steady.

"So moral," Iris spat. "Do you really think all that money Carolyn gave you over the years was hers? Or that trust fund you inherited from your slut of a mother came from *her* meager earnings?"

Harrison went cold.

"You built your empire on dirty money, too, you filthy bastard."

"Not knowingly."

But Iris was past hearing his words. Rage nearly choked her. "I put up with the humiliation of his infidelity all these years. I gave him two strong, *legitimate* sons. I *won't* let you take their inheritance away."

"I told you, I don't want it."

"He can kill me this time, but I won't let a bastard take away all I've worked for."

The cold washed through him. "This time?"

She rushed past him and flung open the door. Jamie stepped protectively in front of him, but it wasn't necessary. Iris climbed into her car and started the engine.

Jamie watched as Iris tore out of the parking space, narrowly avoiding an accident with another car, and sped away. "Wicked stepmother is right. Get your stuff. We need to leave."

This time echoed in his head. Was it really a

leap to think Iris might have been behind his kidnapping all those years ago?

"Move it, Harrison!"

Still considering the implications, he followed Jamie into the bedroom, where she pulled off her T-shirt without hesitation and grabbed a clean one from the bag. If she believed the danger was that imminent, he wasn't going to argue with her. Nor would he ogle her trim, lithe figure.

Harrison stripped off his own shirt and donned his clothes nearly as quickly. "I wish there was time for a shower."

"There isn't," she told him flatly. "In case you didn't notice, Iris isn't the most stable marble in the bag."

"Quaint."

Jamie tossed everything into her bag except the suit he'd replaced on its hanger. "Harrison, she hates you. What do you think will happen when Lyle sees her? You carry the luggage and I'll take the suit. We need to put distance between us and this place right away."

And she wanted to load him down so she'd have a hand free to go for her gun, he realized. She strapped a second gun to her ankle and added a knife. With a last look around, Jamie headed for the door. Ignoring the car, she started walking at a brisk pace.

"That is one crazy, dangerous, paranoid family you've got there, Harrison. They probably have tracking devices on each of their cars. If I hadn't been so tired last night I'd never have touched Gordon's."

"Then we never would have known."

"What?"

"I think Iris was behind my kidnapping as a boy."

Her step faltered. She muttered something under her breath.

"Where are we going?" he asked.

"See that pancake place a couple of blocks down?"

He followed the direction of her gesture. "The one with all the cars circling the parking lot?"

"The more, the better. We can get lost in a crowd."

"Carrying all this?"

Her lips lifted. "Even with all this. I'll call a car rental place to pick us up. We can have breakfast while we wait."

Breakfast. His stomach rumbled assent. "You probably should call the motel and tell them we checked out."

"I'll do that, too."

"Then what?"

"Then we find Kirsten Parsons and shake some answers out of her."

"I like that idea."

THERE WAS A WAIT for a table, so Jamie left Harrison with the bags and went outside to make her calls so she could watch the motel's driveway. Harrison was an alpha male used to making decisions and being in charge, yet he'd followed her lead without hesitating.

He hadn't mentioned last night even once.

Nor had he paid any attention when she'd changed clothes right in front of him. He'd treated her as an equal, as a partner. He'd called her G.I. Jamie and made it sound like a compliment. And when she'd broken down like some helpless female, he'd made her feel protected and safe.

What was she going to do about him? Hadn't she learned a long time ago that there was no safety except what she made for herself? Trusting Harrison was foolish. He was practically married.

To a woman who was carrying another man's baby.

Jamie closed her eyes against a stab of jealousy. Her reaction to him was far scarier than being hunted by someone in the DiMarko family. Harrison was becoming far too important to her. He confused her with those warm looks and small touches. He couldn't be interested in someone like her. There could only be one outcome to this situation.

Harrison had a table by the time she went back inside. Belatedly she realized she had stared at the entrance to the motel without seeing a thing. Iris could have returned with an army and she wouldn't have noticed. Harrison was ruining her edge.

IT WAS LATE AFTERNOON by the time they got a rental car and located Kirsten's apartment complex.

The first two times Jamie had Harrison circle the block to watch for trouble. The next four times it was to locate an on-the-street parking space. In the crowded District of Columbia, those were few and far between. Harrison eventually lucked out when a couple pulled away from the curb. He took the spot quickly even though it was two long city blocks from where they wanted to be. They walked back to the building, where security was seriously lacking. A friendly, middle-aged man let them in with a smile as he left. No one challenged them as they went to the fourth-floor unit designated by her mailbox inside the dark lobby.

"Now what?" Harrison asked as they skipped the decidedly decrepit elevator and used the stairs.

"We knock and then we find out how good my lock-picking skills are."

He raised his eyebrows. "What if someone's home?"

"I doubt either of them will open the door for us if that's the case. If I was Kirsten I'd be in Alabama, North Dakota or Italy. Any place but here."

"Alabama?"

Jamie shrugged. "Someplace unexpected, but I never underestimate the stupidity of people. She could be inside making an early dinner thinking all is well with her world."

"Someone is making dinner." The hall was empty but reeked of cabbage and onions.

Since she wasn't particularly adept at picking locks, Jamie was thankful that this was an older building and that the landlord hadn't gotten around to replacing all the cheap dead bolts. Harrison waited to one side while Jamie rapped briskly on the door. There was no sound from inside. After several minutes she looked up and down the empty hallway and fished out her tools.

For no reason at all that she could see, Harrison reached out and twisted the door handle. It opened with frightening ease. He appeared as startled as she was.

"Stand back. It could be booby-trapped."

"Okay, *that's* paranoia." But he took a respectful step back as she gently kicked the door open farther.

It came up against something and stopped. So did Jamie. The smell hit her just as she saw the graceful curve of a woman's leg. Harrison muttered a low oath as she drew her weapon.

The woman on the floor of the living room was long past disturbing. Her spill of blond hair was matted with the drying red blood that had soaked into the once-neutral carpeting. Apparently, she'd let someone into the apartment and turned her back on them. As with Tony and Carolyn, the killer had only needed one shot to end her life.

"Watch where you step. And don't touch anything." The words were automatic. Sick to her stomach, Jamie closed her eyes against roiling nausea. The smell of death clung to the room.

Harrison's hand on her shoulder held her in place. "Let's go. Kirsten isn't going to tell us anything now."

"This isn't Kirsten. This is Elaine."

Harrison waited. Jamie strove for control. "She was the other woman with us Friday night."

His eyes narrowed and he studied the body. He asked softly, "The dancer in the white outfit that spilled the drink?"

"Yes."

"Then no one died in the farmhouse?"

Jamie shook her head, moving past Elaine. "So it appears."

Again, he stopped her. "Where are you going?"

"To see if she's the only corpse." Obviously, that possibility hadn't crossed his mind.

"What if someone is still in here?"

Jamie should have thought of that. She shook off his hand. "Wait here."

Harrison swore softly, and of course he followed her down the dark hall, but he waited while she cautiously checked out the bathroom, pulling back the shower curtain before crossing to the first room. She judged this to be the smaller of the two bedrooms. The messy jumble of clothing scattered about the room and falling off hangers in the open closet made it hard to tell whose room it was.

The larger room was equally messy. Clothing and makeup were everywhere, but no more bodies, living or dead.

"Not much for housework, were they?" he said.

Jamie didn't respond. Relieved not to find

Kirsten dead as well, Jamie picked up a discarded blouse to cover her hand and started searching the master bedroom.

"What are you looking for?"

"I'll know when I find it."

Harrison scowled, surveying the mess. "It looks to me like someone already searched."

"I don't think so. Cover your hands with something so you don't leave prints and help me pull this dresser drawer out."

"Why?"

"There may be something taped to the bottom or against the inside back wall that will tell us which one of your charming relatives hired them."

"I wish I could take umbrage with that statement."

When they came up blank, Jamie turned to the closet crammed full of clothes. A soft sound of surprise escaped her lips when she pulled a wad of hundred-dollar bills from the pocket of a pair of black slacks.

Harrison raised his eyebrows. "Okay, that's unexpected."

Jamie flipped through them.

"How much is there?"

"A lot." She replaced the money without counting it all. A black sweater top held even more and there was more yet in another pocket. "The going rate for a contract murder must be higher than I thought."

Staring at the money she kept pulling out and replacing, Harrison shook his head. "You're assuming this is Kirsten's room?"

"Yes. Elaine was an exotic dancer," she stated as if that explained everything. Then seeing his expression, she shrugged. "The other room had costumes on the floor."

"Oh." He'd missed that detail. "So, I gather Kirsten doesn't believe in banks."

"This is probably her emergency stash."

"Should I be flattered to know I'm worth that kind of cash?"

"I doubt you were her only job. Ah, here we

go." On the floor in a shoe box she found four bankbooks and whistled. "You were definitely not her only job."

Harrison looked over her shoulder at the impressive numbers. "With that sort of money, why is she living in a cheap apartment?"

"When we find her, you can ask."

Opening a gym bag, Jamie drew in a sharp breath. Quickly, she sealed the bag shut.

"Was that what it looked like?"

"Plastique explosives and blasting caps," she confirmed. "Come on. I think we've seen enough."

"Why would Kirsten leave explosives and all this cash lying around?"

"Why not? Who's going to look twice at a pair of airheaded women that dress like cheap hookers and live in a place like this? It's probably why they haven't moved uptown."

"So who killed Elaine and why?"

"That's the question, all right."

Jamie crossed to the single nightstand and

rummaged through the drawers. She scowled when she didn't find an address book or a telephone list of any sort. "Do you see anything that might have names and phone numbers?"

"She's probably got them on a PDA or cell phone."

"Good point." About to leave, Jamie hesitated and retraced her steps. Picking up the telephone, she hit Redial.

The phone was answered almost immediately. "Yeah?"

Chilled by the sound of the familiar voice, she replaced the receiver. Harrison cocked his head in question.

"Lyle answered. I guess we can extrapolate which one of your charming relatives hired her."

The bedside phone shrilled, making them both jump. Caller ID showed a number without a name. "I think we'd better get out of here."

"Definitely."

They'd just reached the end of the hall when the front door opened, thudding against

Elaine's leg. Jamie pulled her gun as Kirsten stepped inside.

Her expression went from bewilderment to shock, then horror, grief and rage as she took in the body on the floor. Her lips parted. Her eyes came up. She took in the gun pointed at her, turned and fled.

Harrison was closest to the door. He moved fast, but he had to go around the blood and the corpse. Jamie shoved her gun back under her shirt and followed on his heels. The elevator door closed on Kirsten a split second before he reached it.

"Stairs!"

They raced down the steps only to tangle with an overeager puppy on a leash that was coming upstairs with a friendly young couple. The precious seconds wasted cost them any chance of a quick capture, but Harrison didn't hesitate as they reached the main level. "Take the lobby. I'll cover the garage."

"Harrison, she's armed!"

Jamie's protest was wasted. He continued down the stairs in a run. Torn, Jamie hesitated a second before opening the door to the main lobby. One elevator was on its way back up. The second waited passively. There was no sign of Kirsten and nothing to tell Jamie if she'd gone back up or gone all the way down and sent the elevator up.

Racing to the front entrance, she peered outside. She couldn't risk getting locked out, which limited the area she could see. Kirsten had had plenty of time to leave by either door. Nevertheless, Jamie sprinted to the rear entrance, with the same results. Frustrated, she ran back to the stairwell and nearly collided with the door as it opened and Harrison appeared.

"There was a car leaving the underground garage, but it was too far away. I couldn't tell if it was her or not," he reported.

"She may have doubled back and gone upstairs."

"You want to go up and see?"

Two women approached the back door from the rear parking area. Jamie shook her head. "Too risky. Let's go."

Harrison followed her out through the main entrance. "We left her apartment door open."

"Saves us from having to report the body."

She surveyed the street in both directions, unsurprised that there was no sign of Kirsten.

"The couple on the stairs will remember us," Harrison reminded her.

"I know. It's a risk we'll have to take. I'm more worried that Lyle will show up. If he has caller ID he knows the call originated from Kirsten's phone."

"You think he hired them."

Jamie continued watching the street, but Kirsten had completely disappeared. "Yes, but the question is, hired them to do what? It appears that Kirsten and Elaine blew the house, but I can't figure out why they'd go to such convoluted extremes. Why kidnap you? They could have put a bomb on your car before you ever went to Van Wheeler's place. What was the point in involving Tony and me?"

Harrison considered. "Victor said he was trying to protect me from a rival. Victor could have lied about having me kidnapped. His rival, or someone else, could have found out and changed their orders at the last minute."

"I'd buy that except for Victor's reaction. He'd have to be a better liar than most politicians or I've lost my edge when it comes to reading people."

"I agree. It doesn't feel right."

"But I think one person hired them to do the kidnapping and someone else ordered the hit. It's the only explanation that makes sense." She pulled out into traffic. "Iris did say Victor is changing his will. That would give both your half brothers a strong motive."

"Which also explains why Lyle was so angry when we showed up at the restaurant."

Jamie nodded. "He probably thought we were there because we knew he tried to kill us."

"It all fits," Harrison agreed. "So, what do we do now? Call the police?"

"We still don't have a shred of proof. And if I were Kirsten, I'd be running as fast and as far as I could go. She has to know she's the next one to die. We're back to square one."

Harrison cocked his head. "Which is?"

"It begins and ends with Victor, don't you think?"

"Unfortunately, yes."

Her expression was sympathetic. "We can't pick our relatives."

"You did."

Jamie fell silent for so long Harrison didn't think she was going to say anything else. She was cutting through an expensive neighborhood when traffic came to an unexpected halt. Smoke billowed in a dark, ugly plume, dissipating in the sky overhead. Rescue vehicles littered the street. They couldn't see past all the other cars to know what was burning.

"My parents were in a car crash when I was six."

Harrison turned his attention from the scene to Jamie. There was tension in the tilt of her head and she didn't look at him.

"My dad died on impact. Mom's injuries took a long time to heal. By the time they did, she was addicted to pain pills. We lived with my aunt and her family for a time, but we always knew we were in the way. Mom and her sister had a big fight over her medication one day, and we left. We bounced around a lot after that. Mom was pretty, short and delicate. She looked like a teenager though she wasn't. She went from doctor to doctor to get the drugs she craved and from man to man looking for security. She married Morris when I was eleven."

Her hands gripped the steering wheel with fierce intensity. She never looked at him even once. "I take after my dad. I was always big for my age, tall and gawky."

"I'd have said slender and willowy."

She shook her head. "Thank you, but not at

eleven." She rushed on. "I never liked Morris, but Mom was happy and I didn't see all that much of him. I played a lot of sports so I wasn't home much. Then his business went bad and he started drinking. Turned out he was a mean drunk. I continued to stay away from him as much as I could, but my mom didn't have that option. She was so small that I was afraid he'd kill her, so I tried to protect her and take the brunt of his beatings. I even had the temerity to fight back until I realized he liked that."

"He raped you." Harrison barely controlled the sharp thrust of fury that caused both hands to clench.

Jamie shook her head. Her voice became brittle. "No, he got off on beating us. Mom said we had to put up with it because we needed him. *She* needed him. And she was afraid. She thought the police would arrest her because of the drugs, so she begged me to keep quiet. I did for a while, but things only got worse. Finally I couldn't take any more. I stole some money from him one night and left. I lived on the streets with some other runaways until I met Tony and Carolyn."

"I'm sorry, Jamie."

She shrugged. "It was a long time ago. I don't carry it around with me."

"You'll always carry it around," he told her gently. "The difference is you learned how to cope."

She continued to stare at the street, but what she was looking at wasn't out there. "Tony and Carolyn taught me how."

"I'm glad. I wish we could repay them."

She did look at him then. "We can bring Lyle to justice. Even if that means the sort of justice Victor DiMarko is apt to mete out."

Harrison shook his head. "Lyle is his son."

"Victor has his own code of honor. Carolyn once mentioned that Iris had plastic surgery because Victor beat her so bad."

"He *beat* her?" He couldn't have said why that shocked him, but it did.

"Apparently it was only once, for some sort of infraction, but it's one of many reasons I've never liked him."

"There's never any reason for a man to hit a woman."

"On that, we agree."

"We agree on a whole lot more than that, Jamie."

She looked away. "Don't."

"Don't what?" But he knew. Any hint of physical interest on his part was enough to send her running the other way.

"You're engaged."

"Let me tell you about Zoe."

Jamie held up a hand. "Spare me. If you're going to say she doesn't understand you, save it."

Harrison grinned. "Hardly. Zoe understands me better than anyone else I know. You're going to like her. Hey, I'm serious. She doesn't take prisoners, either. She's my administrative assistant and one of my best friends. When she found herself pregnant and being stalked by a killer, I decided she'd be safer if she took my name and the protection I could offer. Artie and Carter would have made the same offer, I just did it first."

"Uh-huh. So what's changed?"

"You," he told her softly.

Jamie grimaced. "Don't."

He touched her arm lightly. A shiver coursed through her, giving him hope. "I was drawn to you the moment I saw you at Artie's. All those women were stripping down to nothing, yet all I could think was you were the only one I'd like to see dancing in a G-string."

"That's sex." But color deepened in her cheeks.

"It certainly is. I've been attracted to you from the start, but I think we both know there's more to our relationship than that."

"We don't have a relationship."

"Not yet."

"You're engaged."

"I am. And until that changes you're perfectly safe. I just want to put you on notice that when it does change, we're going to take the time to find out if there is more than sex to this attraction."

"Forget it, Trent. Don't even think about breaking your engagement for me."

"Traffic's moving."

"I'm serious, Harrison." She inched the car forward, staying with the line of traffic.

"So am I."

"Maybe it escaped your notice, but I live in California."

"Nope. You'd be amazed at what I notice." He kept the smile from his tone as her blush deepened. "I have a contract with a private jet leasing service. I can run my business from pretty much anywhere."

"I won't let you pressure me. Go get married. Live happy."

He let the slow smile reach his lips. "No pressure, Jamie. And no rush at all. To you it must look like I'm dumping one woman in favor of another."

"You are!" She drew in a sharp breath as they came abreast of the accident scene. "Look!"

Diverted, he followed her gaze as they drove slowly past the accident scene. Several cars were involved, but only one vehicle was burnt and mangled almost beyond recognition. Officials were covering the remains of what appeared to have been a limousine. There were obviously still bodies inside.

"The gas tank must have exploded."

Jamie shook her head. Her voice held a trace of something that could have been fear. "That limo was rigged to explode."

"Okay, that's just paranoia rearing its ugly head again."

"Joseph Cristalini goes everywhere in a long black limo. It's his trademark."

A spike of adrenaline slid into his bloodstream.

"Cristalini lives and works here in D.C. He's your father's biggest rival." The gaze she turned on him definitely held fear. "Think about it,

Harrison. The timing is about right. Kirsten plants the explosives, follows the limo long enough to select her spot and triggers the explosion. She would have arrived back at her apartment right about when wc saw her if she went straight there. Didn't Victor promise he'd be taking care of the problem?"

"You're reaching, Jamie." He wished he believed that, but her certainty was taking hold of him. He was very much afraid she was right.

"I don't believe in coincidence," she told him.

"What about the coincidence of our driving past the car right after it blew up?"

"This is a major artery to the nearest Beltway entrance and convenient to her apartment. It's just lousy timing on our part."

Harrison rubbed his jaw. "That means she's working for Victor."

Jamie's voice was grim. "I suspect she works for whoever pays her."

"Freelance?"

"We'll ask Victor when we see him."

"Then why would she have been working as a serving girl at Victor's last night?"

"Do I look like I have all the answers? Maybe it's her regular job. Maybe she was there to meet Victor without attracting attention. Maybe she and Lyle have a thing and it was her cover. I don't know. All we can do is guess and ask questions."

"So, where are we going now?"

"Back to Victor's, unless you have a better idea."

Did he? Harrison considered calling Ramsey Incorporated and dismissed the idea. If he pitted Ramsey's people against his father's organized crime syndicate, someone was bound to get hurt. He didn't want to involve Artie or Carter for the same reason. On the other hand…

"Do you really think we'll be able to get out of his place a second time?"

She bit at her lower lip, considering.

"Let's call and ask him to meet us on neutral territory."

"I don't know, Harrison. He looked pretty frail last night."

"We can ask."

"All right. Where do you suggest we meet him?"

"There's a steak house in Arlington called Ben's. I know the owner and most of the staff. They have a room off to one side for intimate dinner parties. If it isn't in use, it's a perfect spot to hold a private conversation and still be in a public location. Lend me your cell phone. I'll see if it's available."

It was, so he put the next call on speakerphone to his father. Instead he was routed through to Frank. "Mr. DiMarko can't come to the phone right now. I can take a message."

Harrison looked at Jamie, who shrugged. "All right, Frank. Is Victor well enough to meet me somewhere?"

"Today?"

"If possible."

"You could come here."

"I don't think so. I'd rather not have another discussion about whether I stay or go."

"That was my fault. I misunderstood the situation. Mr. DiMarko says you're calling the shots."

"Reassuring, but I'd still prefer to meet him at Ben's in Arlington. It's—"

"I know the restaurant."

Somehow that wasn't comforting. "Okay. Around three o'clock?"

"Make it three-thirty." Frank recited Jamie's cell phone number back at him. "Can I reach you at this number if he's not able to come?"

"Yes," Harrison confirmed.

"Three-thirty at Ben's in Arlington. I'll let him know."

Harrison disconnected and gazed at Jamie. "That gives us time for lunch. Ben's menu is limited, but the food's good."

"Why not? I've got nowhere else to be at the moment."

THE RESTAURANT WAS CROWDED even though it was late for lunch, but the manager hurried over as soon as he saw Harrison. He ushered them personally into the cozy private room and summoned a waitress so they could eat while they were waiting for Victor DiMarko to show up.

"It's always who you know, huh?" Jamie said.

Harrison smiled. "It never hurts to have connections."

"Or money."

"I didn't grow up with money, you know," he told Jamie after they placed their orders.

"I know. I like that about you."

He smiled. "You like poor people?"

"I like people who know what it means to earn their way. In California, a lot of the people I work for take money and the people who have to work for it for granted. They treat their employees like disposable furniture."

Harrison sat back, watching her. "I know you enjoy being a bodyguard, but if you could do something else with your life, what would you do?"

"I'd be a teacher," she replied promptly. "I'm

building a financial cushion right now. When I have enough money set aside, I'm going back to school to get my degree in physical education. We put so much emphasis on grades and getting a degree that physical education is treated like the bastard child. No offense."

His smile widened. "None taken."

"Children need to learn that physical skills are important, too, and there isn't equal emphasis on that. One of the military's slogans is building strong bodies and strong minds. That's because they get it. The two go together more than most people realize."

Her features glowed as she warmed to a subject that was obviously dear to her heart. Harrison could see that Jamie had given this a great deal of thought. With very little encouragement, he kept her talking through lunch, enjoying her vibrant enthusiasm in the plans she'd been making.

Jamie was an intensely private person, so he was surprised that she was opening up to him so easily. He'd never known anyone like her, tiger fierce and lamb gentle at the same time. The fascinating contradictions made for an incredibly special woman. She had so much love and joy bottled up inside.

He wanted to give her those dreams, to watch how she would change lives. But getting her to accept him as part of her future would be a challenge. She wouldn't let him in without a fight. As soon as she realized how much she was revealing, she'd pull back.

It would be worth the battle. Jamie was worth everything. He'd never been more certain of anything in his life.

She flushed suddenly. "I can't believe I went on and on like this."

"Why not? Sharing is what friends do." He watched her walls snap back into place. "Don't say it," he warned when she started to speak again. "I pick my friends with the same care you use to select your weapons. And I choose you as one of my friends."

She opened her mouth, closed it and opened it once more. The confusion in her eyes didn't mask the surprise and yearning he saw there.

"I told you we'd take things slow. I meant it, Jamie. But on some level you trust me or you wouldn't have told me about your plans, right?"

"I'm not sure I like the way you're able to read me so easily."

He smiled. "My sentiments exactly, but you'll get used to it."

"Cocky, aren't you?"

"I'm a man. We're born that way."

It wasn't a full smile, but it was genuine. "I need to find a ladies' room."

"Back toward the bar on your left."

He stood as she did, once more surprising her. When she would have walked past, he stopped her with a gentle touch. "Don't be afraid of me, Jamie."

This time the smile lit her eyes. "As if."

And to both their surprise, she kissed him

lightly on the cheek. Grinning foolishly, he sat back down. He was still smiling when Lyle walked into the room.

Chapter Ten

"We need to talk."

Tense and alert, Harrison remained seated, knowing that Jamie would return in a few moments. While his half brother looked upset, Lyle didn't appear murderous. Yet. "Have a seat. Where's your bodyguard?"

"Outside. And I'll stand. This won't take long. This is between us."

"Fine."

"I don't like you."

"Uh-huh. You did a fine job conveying that impression."

"I want to know what it will take to make you go away. We're both businessmen. You're something of a success at what you do."

Harrison's lips quirked, but he remained silent.

Lyle's eyes narrowed in clear warning as he puffed up his chest. "What's it going to take to make you go away?" he repeated.

Harrison leaned back in his seat. "Are we talking leave the state or stay away from the family?"

The sound Lyle made was amazingly close to a growl. "I'm not playing games here, Trent. I want you to leave my family alone. State your terms."

"There's real irony here, Lyle, but you won't believe me if I tell you."

"Try me."

Leaning forward, Harrison held his brother's gaze and let his voice go soft with menace of his own. "Take the target off my back," he enunciated. "I'll be perfectly happy to have you and your entire family forget I exist. I don't want a single thing from any of you. I never have."

Lyle scowled. He rocked back on his heels looking puzzled. "I almost believe you."

"It's the truth."

The belligerence faded slowly from Lyle's features. "Dad doesn't see it that way."

"That's his problem."

"He called his lawyer in this morning. Fay says he's changing his will."

"Still his problem. Maybe it's yours, too. I don't know and I don't care. I can't change my genetics or believe me, I would. Finding myself a target because of a rivalry not of my making only reinforces my desire to have nothing at all to do with any of you," he said with a hard stare.

"Forget about Cristalini. The situation's been handled."

"You think blowing up the man's limo is going to put a stop to his people trying to kill me?"

Lyle's eyes narrowed to dangerous slits. "How'd you know about the limo?"

"We passed what was left of it on our way over here." Harrison waited a beat. "After we left Kirsten's apartment."

His brother inhaled sharply. The waitress who'd started to enter backed out and turned away. Harrison continued to hold Lyle's gaze. If his brother was going to explode, it would come any second now.

"You called me from there?"

"We hit Redial on her phone," he agreed. "Did you hire her to kill me?"

There was the smallest flicker of surprise. "No."

"Did you ask Tony Carillo to kidnap me Friday night?"

Temper flooded Lyle's florid cheeks with deep color. "No! I thought you showed up because you found out Dad was dying and wanted a cut."

Harrison believed him. "No cut. No nothing. Tony Carillo told Jamie he was doing a favor for a friend."

Comprehension had Lyle nodding thoughtfully, but his brow was furrowed. "Dad."

"That's what Jamie and I thought, too. That's why we wanted to see him."

Lyle shook his head. "Are you telling me you went to see Dad to ask him if he was trying to kill you? Are you nuts or just stupid?"

"We wanted to know who was behind my kidnapping. It appears that Kirsten was taking money from more than one person. Victor claims he doesn't know anything about the kidnapping." Harrison let his shoulder rise and fall. "I believe him."

Once more the aggression leaked from his brother's face. Lyle rocked back and forth slowly. "The bitch knows better. If she was dealing from two decks, she's a dead person."

"If it wasn't you and it wasn't Victor, who—"

Lyle cut him off. "Cristalini." He uttered the name like an oath.

"I don't think so."

Anger returned once more. "What are you suggesting?" Lyle demanded.

"Get your blood pressure checked before you have a stroke, Lyle. Like I said, one person arranged my kidnapping to keep me safe, another person hired Kirsten to create a different outcome."

Lyle swore and started to turn. "I'll take care of the situation."

"You may not get that option."

He stopped and spun back. "Why not?"

"Kirsten's roommate is dead, execution-style, just like the Carillos. It appears she knew the person and let him in. When she turned her back, she was killed. We had a quick look around. Kirsten came in and saw us standing there. She took off leaving enough cash to choke an elephant and a bag of explosives in her bedroom closet. Now, if I were you, I'd be working on an unshakable alibi for the past twenty-four hours, because the police are going to have a lot of questions once they hit that Redial on her phone and it goes straight to you again. Were you sleeping with her?"

Lyle swore steadily in two languages without once repeating himself. "I owe you one."

"No, you don't." But his brother was already vanishing from the room.

The waitress appeared so quickly she must have been standing outside waiting. "Is everything all right, Mr. Trent?"

"No, Holly, but I'm working on it. Would you bring me some coffee?"

"Right away."

The coffee came but Jamie didn't. Harrison wasn't sure how long he and Lyle had talked, but he knew Jamie should have returned by now.

"Holly, would you check the ladies' room and see if my friend is okay?"

"Certainly."

The longer he sat there, the more his agitation grew. Pulling out a sheaf of bills, he laid them on the table and stood. What if Jamie had run into Lyle as he was leaving?

Holly was exiting the hall that led to the bathrooms when he reached the bar area. One look at her expression and Harrison knew he'd been right to worry.

"Mr. Trent, she isn't in there. Kevin says two women left some time ago. One of them appeared to be ill."

The manager hurried over. "Mr. Trent, there's a phone call for you. The caller says it's urgent."

Harrison followed him to the hostess's podium and picked up the telephone. "Trent."

"If you want to see Jamie Bellman alive again you'll come alone to Big Al's Scrap Yard off Regency Lane," a muffled voice told him. "You have forty minutes. If you tell anyone or bring anyone with you, you'll never find her body."

The click echoed in his ear. Harrison dropped the phone and sprinted for the door. Their rental car was still sitting in the lot, but Jamie had the keys. His gaze landed on the silver Aston Martin Iris had been driving earlier. The lone figure in the car sat behind the wheel holding a cell phone to her ear.

Iris jerked her head up in shock as he flung open the driver's door.

"Where's Jamie?"

"What?"

"No games, Iris. Where's Jamie?"

"I don't know."

He held on to his temper by a thread. Fear turned her flawless skin a mottled red. She closed the cell phone and stared at him.

"Open the trunk!"

"I didn't take her!"

"Open the trunk and get out of the car or I'll pull you out." He vibrated with suppressed fury.

Her hand shook as she pressed the release and climbed shakily from the car. Harrison grabbed her arm and hauled her around to gaze inside the empty trunk.

"I told you I don't have her."

"What did you do with her?"

"It wasn't me."

"Who, then?" He shook her, barely controlling the rage and fear that filled him.

"Lyle." The name came on a gasp. "He was driving away when I pulled in."

Harrison's heart plummeted. Lyle had come to talk with him as a diversion while he had someone spirit Jamie away. But why? What would Lyle want with Jamie? "Was there a woman with him?"

Iris quailed. "No. Just his bodyguard. I saw him get in the car and they drove off."

"The staff inside said she left the restroom with another woman."

Her face suddenly blanched. Her mouth went slack. "Fay. Oh God, it was Fay."

That rocked him back. "Why would Fay take Jamie?"

A fat tear dripped from her eye. "She's upset. She believes Victor is going to cut her and her brothers out of the will because of you."

"What does that have to do with Jamie?" But even as he asked, he knew. Jamie had been taken to get to him.

"I don't know," Iris sobbed.

"Did Victor tell Fay he was going to change his will in my favor?"

"No, but she says he's obsessed with you."

Cold iced his body. Iris flinched.

"Where did she go?"

"I don't know. Fay isn't always…rational. I tried to tell her everything would be all right. Victor would never cut out his own children, but she blames you for so much."

Harrison refrained from shaking the woman. "What have I ever done to her?"

"When I first learned about Victor's…indiscretion with your mother, I…well, I reacted badly."

"You had me kidnapped when I was fourteen."

She flinched. "Yes. But I wasn't going to hurt you! I wanted Victor to suffer. I was going to make him pay through the nose to get you back. Only he found out what I'd done. He… I've never feared him before, but I thought he was going to kill me that day." She touched her face in remembered pain. "He nearly did. He was furious."

She began to sob, harsh, deep sobs. Yet all Harrison felt were the minutes sliding past.

"Fay loves me. We've always been close, and she was angry when she saw what Victor did to me. She blamed you for what happened."

"She's insane."

"No! No, she's just…different." But the protest rang weak and frightened.

"Then what are you doing here, Iris?"

"I've been keeping an eye on her. I had a tracking device on her car."

"Had."

Iris shuddered and pulled a small object from her pocket. "I found it over there on the ground. She must have found it. I thought I could stop her from doing something stupid."

Fear settled in his gut. "Where did she take Jamie, Iris?"

"I don't know!"

The caller's voice had been muffled. It could have been Fay, or it could have been anyone. Frustration and fear chewed on his soul.

"The caller said Big Al's Scrap Yard."

She swayed. "Oh God."

"What?"

"It's an auto recycling plant. Victor…he's used it in the past to…"

Panic threatened to swallow him whole. "To get rid of bodies he doesn't want turning up?" he pushed out past the tension choking him.

She managed a nod.

"Let's go."

"Victor will kill me!"

He looked her straight in the eye. "So will I if anything happens to Jamie."

The force of his words surprised even him. Iris blanched.

"Get in the car."

She obeyed despite the trembling that made her movements jerky. All traces of her earlier haughty arrogance were gone as she put her car in gear and pulled into traffic with erratic movements.

Harrison couldn't summon any sympathy for her. He kept picturing Jamie at Fay's hands and he could barely hold his terror at bay. They'd overlooked Fay, and weren't the quiet ones the people who were always overlooked in books and movies?

"She was behind my kidnapping Friday night, wasn't she?"

"No." Her frightened gaze begged for understanding. "That was me, again."

He swallowed an oath.

"I had no choice! Fay found out her father was going to attend your wedding. I overheard her call Cristalini. She told him if he wanted revenge on Victor's youngest child, she could hand him you and…and Victor as well. I was terrified. I knew Frank wouldn't let Victor walk into an ambush, but if they killed you…" She shuddered, her fear tangible.

"You have to see Victor would have blamed me. He would have killed me this time! So I called Tony. I asked him to arrange for you to be protected until well after the wedding. Then I let Frank know anonymously that Cristalini knew about you and was going to hit the church." Her voice cracked on a sob. "You can see I had to protect Fay. She's my only daughter! I thought I could talk to her, make her see what a dangerous game she was playing, only she… She isn't well."

"She's insane."

"No! She's always been…different. High-strung. I've tried to take care of her."

"You mean cover for her."

"You don't understand. She resented Victor's affair. She knew how much he hurt me and she hated that he cared about you. She honestly believes he is planning to favor you over his real flesh and blood."

Harrison didn't point out that he was real flesh and blood as well. He was too worried about Jamie in the hands of a nutcase. "So you killed Tony and Carolyn?"

"No! Of course not!"

His fear grew. "Then Fay did."

"I don't know." She began to cry again. "She's

always wanted to be tough like that awful Kirsten and her sister."

"Her sister?"

"Elaine. The exotic dancer. Fay was fascinated by the pair of them. She always said they were tough and lived by their own rules. Victor respects toughness. Fay's only ever wanted his approval, and he treats her like a favored pet or something. She wishes she'd been born a boy so she could inherit the business."

Harrison shook his head. Could these people be any more twisted? "Tell me about the scrap yard. What's the setup there?"

"I don't know. I've never been there. What are you going to do?"

"I'm going to get Jamie back."

"Why do you care? She's just a bodyguard."

He swallowed an angry retort, remembering Jamie's earlier words about people who lacked empathy for the working class. He could point out several things to her, but they would fall on deaf ears.

He had the gun Jamie had given him, and while

he knew he could use it if he had to, the odds of him actually hitting anyone if he had to fire it were slim. Fortunately, Fay wouldn't know that. Harrison knew how to run a bluff. He figured that was his best option. "Tell me something, Iris. Is Fay crazy enough to kill you as well?"

"Stop calling her crazy! I'm her mother. Of course she won't hurt me."

"I hate to tell you this, but crazy people kill their mothers all the time. You've said she isn't playing with a full deck, so I want to know how close we can get to her before she loses it."

"Let me talk to her. I'll make her see reason."

"You do that. Because if she hurts Jamie, I'll see to it she pays."

"You sound just like your father."

For a moment he was taken aback. Then he nodded. "Then you won't have any illusions about what will happen if you fail, will you?"

GROGGY, JAMIE STRUGGLED to think. Darkness encased her. She tried to move her hands and couldn't. There was pain, and she could barely feel her fingers. She couldn't move her feet, either.

Fighting panic, she forced her sluggish brain to assess the situation. Sweat poured from her body. The air was stifling. Each breath was painful. She wanted to vomit. Winning the battle with her stomach took nearly all her effort. Her cheek scraped against rough fabric. Her breaths became pants. She forced them to slow.

A trunk. She was trapped inside the trunk of a car. Why was she in a trunk?

Fear reasserted itself. Where was she? Why couldn't she remember?

She battled the fear, tasting panic at its core. If only she could breathe. She was baking alive in here. She had to get out. Think!

All car trunks have emergency releases. Find it. The car wasn't moving, but with her hands tied behind her back, how was she going to do that? Even her ankles were bound tight enough to cut off circulation. If she'd been wearing a gag she'd probably be dead. The heat was suffocating her.

Never mind. Arch your back and feel for the latch.

Where was Harrison? How had she let someone take her like a rookie? Who? And why was she still alive?

Jamie forced her breathing to slow. She fought the rising panic.

Think. Don't panic.

The words became her mantra. *Find the safety release. Open the trunk and let in some air in before you pass out again.* Did she still have her knife strapped to her leg? She couldn't tell.

It doesn't matter right now. Find the release!

There was a loud thud against the trunk. Jamie jerked, startled.

"Hey. You still alive in there?"

The trunk abruptly opened. Sunlight blinded her. Jamie sucked in the hot afternoon air greedily, her mouth so dry there was no saliva.

"Awake, are we?"

Despite her watering eyes, Jamie tried to focus on the blurred face peering down at her.

"If your boyfriend could see you now. You're a mess. And you stink."

She knew that voice. Her confused brain struggled to put a name to the voice.

"You should have died at the farmhouse, you know. It would have saved us both a great deal of trouble. Kirsten will pay for that as soon as I'm done using her."

"Fay?" Jamie's voice cracked.

"Of course, Fay. Mousy, quiet Fay, Daddy's little princess." She spat the words as though they were vile. "Well, Daddy's about to learn a thing or two about princesses. We can grow up to take over the kingdom."

The venom in the woman's voice pierced the fog shrouding her brain. Fay DiMarko was going to kill her. Jamie tried to reach for the knife sheath at her ankle.

"Looking for this?"

Light glinted off the blade Fay was waving in her face.

"I have all of your little toys, Jamie. It's quite

a collection. Too bad I have to kill you. If you're proficient with all these weapons, you might have served me well. Sadly, you only have one role here. Yelp in pain when I cut you, and die when I shoot you. Simple, yes?"

Jamie struggled harder against her bonds, panic clawing her insides.

"Struggle all you want, you aren't getting out of those knots. I'm good at knots. I'm good at a lot of things. I've been studying. I'm already a crack shot and I know all the pressure points. Want a demonstration?"

She reached in and grabbed Jamie's arm. A scream tore past her lips as Fay twisted the skin, sending searing pain up the arm.

"Good. Maybe I won't cut you after all. A scream like that should control him, don't you think? And blood is so hard to clean off the carpeting. Daddy's little bastard should be here any time now."

Harrison. Fay was using Jamie to lure Harrison. And he'd come for her, just as he'd gone to the church for Zoe. Chivalry was his middle name. She had to think.

"Fortunately, I was standing right there when the bastard called and told Frank where to find you. I knew Daddy was tied up with the doctor, but I was afraid he'd show up before I could get both of you away from the restaurant."

There would be no rationalizing with Fay. Jamie recognized the fanaticism in her tone. Fay might be scary nuts, but she wasn't stupid.

"I was on the verge of sending a waitress in to get you when you obligingly went to the bathroom. I have to say, for a bodyguard, you were certainly easy to take down."

Chagrined at the truth of that, she mouthed one word. "How?"

"Easy. As you came out of the stall I hit you with the Taser. Then I gave you enough joy juice to make you docile so I could help my sick *friend* outside. You might think someone saw me put you in the trunk, but I'm afraid no one paid any attention to us. Did the joy juice leave you feeling frisky, Jamie?"

She reached down and squeezed Jamie's breast hard. "Too bad you aren't my type. Kirsten and Elaine said you're either a prude or you like women. Which is it, huh, Jamie?"

"Elaine's dead."

"Of course she is. I shot her." Her eyes narrowed to vicious slits. "But how did you know that?"

Jamie lifted her chin. She needed to keep Fay distracted while she tried to work her hands free. "We found her body."

Fay tapped Jamie's knife against the edge of the trunk. "Well, now. You're just full of surprises, aren't you? How did you know where they lived?"

"It wasn't difficult. Do you really think your father won't figure it out if you kill Harrison?"

"Don't you worry about Daddy. He's dying and I'm going to help him along. My brothers, too. There's going to be an explosion. So tragic. One big bang, and I will be the grieving survivor of a horrible family tragedy. And the only one left to fill Daddy's shoes."

"You're going to kill your mother, too?"

Fury burned in eyes that Jamie now saw were widely dilated.

"Of course not. Mommy's a weakling, but I'll take care of her."

Abruptly Fay grabbed Jamie by the hair and jerked her to her knees inside the trunk. Jamie cried out at the sudden pain. Fay was amazingly strong.

"What? You don't think I can do it?"

The backhand slap sent Jamie tumbling. Her head slammed against something hard and she wrenched her back as she fell into the trunk again. Blood dripped from a gash on her cheek.

Fay peered at the large gemstone ring on her finger and grinned evilly. "Yes, that *is* better. Just a little blood to keep him in line. It shouldn't be too much longer now. The bastard better hurry. I'm getting bored. You won't like me when I'm bored."

"I don't…like you now," she managed.

Fay threw back her head and laughed. The maniacal sound sent Jamie's heart racing. Fay wasn't just insane. Unless Jamie missed her guess, the woman was higher than a kite on something.

Her eyes swept what she could see of their surroundings. It looked like a graveyard for old cars. Vehicles of all shapes and sizes sat baking in the merciless afternoon sun, which glinted off broken windshields and rusting chrome. Birds circled lazily overhead. There had to be something nearby that Jamie could use to defend herself.

"I knew I liked you," Fay chortled. "You're no wimp. Not like my mother. She should have ordered the bastard killed the minute she found out about him instead of trying to kidnap him and make my father pay. I'd have sent dear old Daddy his bastard child's head in a box. Then I—oh, good. Here comes a car."

The crunch of tires as the car approached

drew Jamie's gaze to the open path past the stack of old vehicles. She recognized the car the same time Fay did.

Fay's oath was harsh and violent. "What's *she* doing here? She's going to ruin everything!"

Jamie knew she wouldn't get a better chance. Struggling to her knees, she pulled frantically at the cord biting into her wrists. Blood flowed down her hands as her skin was rubbed raw, but the knots held. Fay had known exactly what she was doing.

The thought was terrifying.

The silver Aston Martin came to a halt and Iris climbed out. She was no longer the cool, composed woman Jamie had met. Disheveled and red-eyed, Iris showed every one of her years and then some.

"What are *you* doing here?" Fay demanded of her mother.

"Fay, you have to stop." Iris's voice quavered.

"Get back in the car, Mother."

Jamie's heart sank. Iris didn't seem to sense

the danger. Fay was unpredictable and dangerous.

Iris took a step forward. "Fay, Victor will kill you."

"No, he won't. He's the one who's going to die. You're weak, but I'm not. I know exactly what I'm doing. All Daddy cares about are his precious sons. We both know that. And look where it got him. Lyle's a muscle-headed bully who couldn't run things if he had to, while Gordon fancies himself an architect, too good to get his hands dirty anymore."

She swung her arms wide, the sun glinting off the knife in her hand. "He never even considered me, but I'm the one who can run things. I'm more than just his little princess."

"Fay, don't."

"He was going to give away our birthright! To his bastard son no less!" Her voice rose in pitch along with the fury that sent spittle flying from her lips. "Don't you have any pride? Did he beat it out of you all those years ago?"

Jamie struggled vainly with her bonds until motion to one side of the car drew her gaze. Her heart hammered wildly. Harrison! He was working his way toward her from the side, but he was out of cover. He would have to cross the wide-open expanse of dirt to reach her. He should still be armed, but he'd never fired a gun before. Fay was quick and she had a gun tucked in the front waistband of her slacks. She would cut him down in an instant if he didn't incapacitate her first.

"You don't know that," Iris was protesting as she continued toward her daughter. "Your father isn't going to give Harrison anything." Iris's voice was agitated. Her gaze kept straying as if she were looking for something—or someone. Any minute now she'd see Harrison. "Trent doesn't want anything from us."

"Stop where you are, Mother!"

Iris stopped, visibly trembling.

"Do you think I'm stupid? All that power. Of course the bastard wants to run Daddy's empire."

"Fay, you don't even know what changes Victor plans to make to his will," Iris pleaded.

"It doesn't matter. He wouldn't consider turning things over to me. We both know women only count for one thing with him. Who knows that better than you?"

"Fay, please!"

"Get in the car and leave, Mother. I'll deal with you later."

Iris's gaze fastened on Harrison. He was in the open now with nothing between him and Fay. Fay followed that gaze, whipping around in shock.

"Harrison, run!" Jamie's voice came out a strangled croak of sound, but he heard her. He shook his head, gazing right at her.

"It's okay, Jamie, I'm not going to leave you."

He stopped, staring right at Fay. "I'll make a deal with you, Fay. Let Jamie go with your mother."

Iris started sobbing, great tearing sobs that rent the air.

"The only one you want to punish is me," Harrison told her. "And I'm right here. Let Jamie and your mother walk away."

"You aren't calling the shots," Fay snarled, her hand going for the gun at her waist. "I am. Shut up, you weak fool," she ordered her mother.

Iris shook her head and continued moving in Fay's direction. Fay jerked back toward her and pulled the trigger.

The harsh sound startled the flock of birds. They took to the air with shrill cries of alarm. Iris crumpled on the hard-baked earth and didn't move. The sudden silence was shocking.

Fay started to turn back toward Harrison, but Jamie threw herself at Fay. She knew the woman was too far away, but she created the only diversion she could offer Harrison. She tipped from the trunk and landed on the ground at the other woman's feet. Fay spun, kicking her hard in the ribs.

A shot filled the air, much louder than the first. For a heartbeat that lasted an eternity, no one moved. Then Fay sprawled facedown in the dirt beside Jamie.

Harrison ran to her side, pausing to kick the gun away from the fallen woman's fingers before stepping around Fay to lift Jamie tenderly, protectively. "I'm sorry, Jamie. I'm so sorry."

Her gaze fell on the man walking slowly toward them, a gun in the hand at his side.

"I'm sorry, too," Victor DiMarko said sadly.

His bodyguard ran forward from yet another direction. Fay continued to writhe on the ground, making low, keening noises. "You okay, Mr. DiMarko?"

"No, Frank. I'm not okay. Cuff her and disarm her." He stepped past his daughter and crossed to where his wife lay still and silent.

Frank swore under his breath. He handed Harrison the knife, which he'd taken from Fay without moving his eyes from where Victor crouched beside his wife.

"Is she—?"

"No, Frank. Fay's an excellent shot. Iris needs

a doctor, but she'll live. Call Farncowitz. Tell him to send an ambulance here right away. Farncowitz owns a private clinic," he added for Harrison's benefit.

Jamie whimpered past clenched teeth when Harrison cut the cords, returning circulation to her swollen hands and feet.

"I know you never wanted anything from me, Harrison," Victor continued quietly. "I admire that, almost as much as I regret it. Still, you'll take this gift. Take Jamie and go. I'll see you're both kept out of this."

Harrison dropped the bloody cords he'd cut from her arms and legs and gazed at his father without releasing her. "You can't cover this up, Victor."

"Actually, I can." He gazed at them sadly, a frail old man in a wasted body. "Lyle, Gordon and I can handle the situation. Assuming I can find Gordon."

"He went to Vegas," Harrison told him. "To marry Liz Sylor."

Victor's gaze softened in approval. "Did he, now?"

"He wants to be an architect."

"Yes, I know."

"I told him I'd help."

The sad old eyes gleamed approval. "I'm glad, son. He'll need a brother when this is over. He and Lyle never did get along."

"Ambulance is on the way, Mr. DiMarko."

"Thank you, Frank."

Harrison hesitated. "I have a friend who's a lawyer."

The smile reached Victor's lips. "So do I. And I pay him a great deal to clean up my messes, but I appreciate your offer."

Harrison shrugged.

"I know this changes nothing, Harrison, but I want you to know that I loved your mother. If she'd have had me, I'd have found a way to make it work between the two of us. Unfortunately, Iris knew that. I suspect Fay did as well. It's why she hated you and the Carillos so much."

Tense and silent, Harrison stared at his father.

He sighed. "Frank, take Jamie and my son to the Kingstreet house. Stay with them. Have Dr. Mercer meet them there."

"That won't be necessary," Harrison told him quickly.

"I'm afraid it will. I need the two of you out of the way for the next twenty-four hours until the dust settles. You're guests, not prisoners. You'll be free to leave tomorrow. Frank, they have my word on that."

Frank looked as deeply troubled as Harrison. He had taped Fay's hands behind her back. Her side was covered in blood and she struggled weakly to sit up. "What about Ms. DiMarko, sir?"

"I can handle my daughter, Frank."

"Yes, sir. Come with me please, Mr. Trent. Ms. Bellman."

Jamie gazed at him. "Harrison?"

He lowered his eyes to hers slowly. "It's okay, Jamie. I trust him."

Harrison scooped her into his arms and stood, cradling her against his chest and ignoring her protest. His gaze returned to his father. "Thank you. For both gifts."

Victor DiMarko smiled freely for the first time. Years fell from his expression. "You're welcome, son."

Chapter Eleven

The Kingstreet house proved to be a graceful Colonial on an acre of wooded property over-looking the Accokeek River. They stopped along the way to pick up their luggage from the rental car and to buy supplies that included bandages and some cold water for Jamie to drink.

Harrison considered walking away more than once, but Jamie was in no shape to walk anywhere. He was mildly alarmed when his feisty warrior made no protest and allowed him to clean and bandage her injuries without fuss. She didn't even protest when he kissed her forehead. After gulping down half a bottle of water, she fell into a fitful doze nestled in his arms. He wondered if she realized how much she'd come to trust him.

Harrison had no illusions. Once she was recovered, Jamie would pull back on every level. That didn't matter. They had time now. He could be patient and relentless when he wanted something, and he very much wanted Jamie in his life.

She was alive. Her physical injuries were minor and would heal. The gash on her cheek had already stopped oozing blood, although a bruise was forming. But the deep shadows under her eyes told him it was the internal healing they were all going to have to deal with.

"What do you think Victor will do, Frank?"

The other man met his eyes in the rearview mirror as he turned onto a wide, twisting driveway.

"Mr. DiMarko handles his family personally. He does what has to be done. It's why he's the one who pulled the trigger on his daughter and not me."

He pulled up in front of the sprawling Colonial and shut off the engine. "Dr. Farncowitz runs a private clinic. Mr. DiMarko recently learned Fay had a drug problem and was making arrangements to have her treated there. Mrs. DiMarko has been doing a good job covering for her, but he'll see to it they both get help."

Harrison didn't ask what sort of help.

"Are we there yet?" Jamie asked sleepily, roused by their voices.

"We just pulled in."

She eyed the sprawling structure. "House, huh?"

Harrison forced a lighter tone. "Mansion sounds so pretentious."

Tiredly, she smiled. "At least it isn't a castle. Drafty places, castles."

"No moat," he pointed out.

"So probably no dragon."

"The dragon's in restraints," he told her flatly.

"Good."

Jamie climbed stiffly from the car before he could stop her. He hurried around to scoop her up once more.

"Put me down. I can walk."

"I like carrying you."

"I am not paying for your massage therapist or your chiropractor."

"No problem. I keep one of each on payroll," he deadpanned.

"Of course you do."

Frank moved ahead to open the door and disarm the alarm system. Then he began ferrying groceries and suitcases inside. Harrison eyed the rooms approvingly. The house was furnished in a comfortable style, and soft pastel colors made it surprisingly warm and inviting.

"Beats Victor's mansion hands down," Jamie commented.

Harrison set her on the couch and nodded agreement.

"Why are we here, Harrison?"

"Victor wants us out of the way while he spins the story to his advantage."

"Three people are dead, his wife and daughter are wounded and Fay's insane. How does he think he's going to spin something like that? He can't cover it up."

"No, he can't."

Her gaze filled with sympathy and regret. Harrison touched her unmarked cheek gently. "I'll carry the bags upstairs. Sit here and relax. Frank's going to grill some chicken for dinner."

"How long are we going to stay?"

"Tonight," he told her firmly. By morning they'd know how Victor had decided to handle things.

Despite the cheerful kitchen, the three of them picked at the meal Frank had prepared. The bodyguard staked his claim on the maid's quarters on the first floor and disappeared inside shortly after helping them clean up.

Jamie stopped Frank from calling a doctor. Since her color had returned and she seemed stronger now that the drug was wearing off, Harrison agreed.

Gazing at the closed door of the maid's quarters, she shook her head. "Scary guy."

"He not only knows where the bodies are buried, he probably helped kill most of them," Harrison agreed.

He rested a hand on her thigh as she curled beside him on the couch. The nightly news carried the first reports of the exotic dancer murdered in her D.C. apartment. A search was under way for the dead woman's roommate, her sister, Kirsten Parsons. There were scenes of the bomb squad removing what the reporter called a suspicious bag containing possible explosives from the apartment.

"Could they possibly leave out any more information?" Jamie asked.

"Let's be grateful for small favors."

"Is he going to let Kirsten take the fall for Elaine's murder?"

Harrison shrugged.

"I notice there was no mention of your kidnapping."

"Carter Hughes isn't just my friend. He's very good at covering my backside."

"Must be a full-time job."

He smiled. "Only since I met you."

Jamie sniffed. "Your relationship to Victor is probably going to come out, you know."

"I guess I should call Carter and alert him." He eyed the phone on the table across from them.

"I'll go upstairs and give you some privacy."

He laid a restraining hand on her arm and felt a tiny quiver run through her. "Stay. I don't need privacy from you."

Her gaze was clouded, but she nodded and remained seated. He rose and crossed to the telephone.

"You want to tell me what's going on?" Carter demanded as soon as he heard Harrison's voice. "I just had Victor DiMarko's lawyer on the phone telling me an outrageous tale. He claims you're DiMarko's biological son."

"True."

There was a beat of silence. "He also claims DiMarko's daughter found out and had you kidnapped so she could murder you to keep you from getting a share of his wealth."

"Close enough."

This time the silence was pregnant. Carter's voice was low and soft when he spoke again. "Fay DiMarko just checked into a private clinic that caters to drug and mental problems. I assume this is the same daughter?"

"As far as I know, he had only the one."

His friend swore softly. "Talk to me, Harrison."

"Not over the phone. I did warn you that you'd need to finagle a few things."

"Harrison, this isn't a few things and we are way past the finagling point. You're related to a known crime boss. How do you want me to handle this?"

"Follow DiMarko's script. I have no connection to the family other than an unavoidable biological one. I have no interest in the

DiMarkos or their affairs. Keep a lid on the kidnapping."

"And the reason your wedding didn't take place?"

"Is between Zoe and me. Full stop."

Carter muttered something too low to hear. Harrison offered Jamie a wry shrug. "Use your discretion, Carter. It's why I pay you the big bucks."

"Remember that when you get my bill. You *are* okay, right?"

"Yes. What about Zoe?"

"I haven't spoken with her, but Mark Ramsey has people covering her."

"Good. I'll call her later."

"I'm sure she'd appreciate it."

He ignored the sarcasm in Carter's voice.

"What *are* you going to do about the wedding?"

"There isn't going to be one."

"Ever? You mean because of the DiMarko connection?"

"Because I realized it was a mistake for both of us," Harrison corrected.

"Well, thank God for that."

Surprised, Harrison frowned. "I thought you liked Zoe."

"I adore Zoe. That's why I'm glad you came to your senses in time."

"Don't tell me *you're* going to pursue her."

Carter snorted. "I've been a lawyer too long to have any interest in the institute of matri-*money*. I just hate to see people I care about making a mistake, no matter how well intended."

"You never said anything."

"What was the point? Artie tried and you weren't listening. I did insist on the prenup, if you'll recall."

"You're a lawyer. That's your bread and butter."

"I do corporate law, remember? And we're off the subject again. What do *you* need right now, Harrison?"

"Eight hours of uninterrupted sleep and a media blackout on my end." He looked at Jamie's battered face. "You might want to have someone who specializes in criminal law on standby in case questions arise."

Carter's voice deepened. "What sort of questions?"

"Later."

"I'll come to you." Determination filled Carter's voice.

"You're a good friend, Carter, but later, counselor. After we've had some sleep."

"We." His voice flattened. "Would this *we* have anything to do with your need for a criminal attorney on standby?"

"I'll call you tomorrow. I need to go now."

"Harrison, don't hang up."

Gently he replaced the receiver. "That went well."

"Did it?" Jamie managed to look amused and serious at the same time.

"Let's go to bed. I'd offer to carry you up

the stairs, but I think we'd both be in trouble if I tried."

She stood quickly and winced as muscles protested. "I can walk for myself."

"Good. Then how about if you carry me?"

"Fool." But her eyes smiled at him.

It wasn't until they reached the upstairs landing that she hesitated. He'd placed her bag in the room across from his. "You took a terrible risk this afternoon, but thank you."

"It's Victor we both have to thank." Gazing into her soft, dark eyes, he knew he was going to take a different risk. "If I kiss you right now, will you slap me?"

For an instant, she froze like a startled deer. Then she shook her head. "No. But it's a bad idea."

"I know."

He waited. She didn't move even when he shaped her face tenderly, lightly stroking the skin beneath her injury with his thumb. A tiny tremor ran through her, giving him hope.

His fingers tangled in her hair as he covered her lips with his own. He expected her to stiffen. Instead an electric jolt ran through him as she parted her lips and kissed him back with welcome hunger. What he'd meant to be a simple kiss exploded in passion.

The slick glide of her tongue over his produced a low rumble of satisfaction in the back of his throat. He deepened the kiss and she strained against him, her arms circling his neck. They fused together, on fire for the taste and feel of each other.

He slid his fingers up her sides, letting them come to rest beneath the fullness of her breasts. Jamie made a soft sound and arched against him. Without thought, he pinned her to the wall and thrust his hips against her yielding softness.

Somehow the remnants of sanity reasserted themselves even as his hand cupped her breast through her shirt and she moaned acceptance. Shakily, he released her, pulling away slightly, but resting his forehead against hers. He cupped her face gently.

Her breathing was coming as fast and hard as his. They sounded as if they'd just run a marathon. For a timeless moment they stood there like that.

"I knew this was a bad idea," she whispered.

His chuckle was hoarse. He withdrew, meeting the desire in her eyes with his own. She lowered her gaze and used both hands to shove against his chest lightly.

Harrison took another step back. "I won't apologize. I've wanted to do that since the first time I laid eyes on you."

"It's just sex." But her dismissive words were shaky at best.

"Jamie, I know all about 'just sex' and the sex between us is going to be fabulously explosive, but we both know there's a whole lot more going on here. You're worthy of being loved. Don't for a minute believe otherwise."

"I don't!"

"I think you do. I think that's why you work so hard to push me away, but I'm not going anywhere. You have the heart of a lioness, Jamie. Fight for us, because I'm sure going to."

"Zoe—"

"Will be the first to wish us well, wait and see."

"You're still engaged."

"Which is the only reason we aren't going to complete what we just started here."

"Stop it!"

He shook his head. "Not going to happen. Go rebuild your walls. You've got all night. I'll scale them again tomorrow. I've waited a long time to find someone like you and I can be amazingly patient."

Her chin rose, jaw set with determination. "And I can raise stubborn to an art form."

Harrison grinned. "Should be fun."

Chapter Twelve

"Harrison! Wake up! Frank's gone."

Harrison came fully awake at the first sound of Jamie's voice. She was up and dressed, her hair damp, obviously from a shower. The bandage was gone from her cheek, which sported a nasty-looking bruise.

"We overslept. It's almost nine-thirty. I went downstairs to make coffee and there was a pot made, but the car's gone and so is Frank. The maid's room doesn't even look like it was slept in."

Harrison slid out of bed. His gaze fell on the dresser, where he'd left his wallet and keys and the gun she'd given him. "Did you take the gun?"

Her eyes widened and she cursed. "No."

"Let me get dressed."

Throwing on clothes, he hurried downstairs after her.

"The good news is that so far I haven't found any sign that the house is rigged to explode," Jamie said.

That staggering possibility hadn't even crossed his mind. "What's the bad news?"

She nodded toward the front window. "There's someone coming."

"That's the car Frank was driving."

"We'll go out the back."

He rested a hand on her arm. "Why? No one's trying to kill us anymore."

"You still have two brothers. I don't see Lyle being very happy with us about now. Let's go."

Harrison shook his head as the car came to a halt out front. "Wait. I trust Victor."

"You're out of your mind!"

"Maybe."

Frank stepped out of the car and reached back inside.

"You're going to get us killed!"

"If Frank wanted to shoot us, he would have done it before he left."

Frank took a bag from the front seat and started for the door.

"Looks like he went shopping." Harrison released Jamie to open the door for the other man. "Everything okay?"

Frank's expression was bleak. "No, but it's going the way Mr. DiMarko wants it to go. I bought stuff for breakfast."

"Where's Harrison's gun?" Jamie demanded.

"It's being disposed of. Mr. DiMarko didn't want what happened to Tony and Carolyn Carillo linked back to the two of you."

Harrison urged Jamie down the hall in Frank's wake. "You talked with Victor?"

"Not directly." He set down the bag and looked at Jamie. "Ms. Bellman, I'm going to reach my hand in my pocket for your cell phone," he told her calmly. "Mr. DiMarko asked me to return the personal items he retrieved from Fay."

"Where are my weapons?"

"Mr. DiMarko disposed of all the items you took from the Carillos' house."

Slowly, Frank withdrew her cell phone and keys and set them on the table in front of her. "This is how it's going down. Fay has been acting irrational and Mr. DiMarko found out she'd started using drugs after hanging with Kirsten Parsons and her sister. He was taking steps to get her help. Mrs. DiMarko was keeping close tabs on Fay. Her daughter resented it."

Frank sighed and pinched the bridge of his nose. "Mrs. DiMarko followed her out to the scrap yard, where she suspected Fay was meeting Elaine and Kirsten to buy more drugs. Some sort of altercation took place and Fay was shot. Mrs. DiMarko was caught in the cross fire between Fay and Kirsten and was wounded."

Harrison admitted the simple logic. However… "Have they found Kirsten?"

"Mr. DiMarko is working on it."

"It doesn't explain Elaine's murder," Jamie pointed out.

"The cops should see it as a falling-out between the two women. We know they found a small stash of drugs in their apartment, so the story will play. Mr. DiMarko is telling the cops he followed Mrs. DiMarko to the scrap yard and arrived in time to see Kirsten leaving the scene."

"This is all going to come apart if Kirsten goes to the police."

"She won't. Leave Kirsten to us."

Harrison felt the ripple of emotion course through Jamie. He shared her concern. Kirsten would never willingly go along with this story. That meant Victor planned to kill her. Could he stop the man?

"Mr. DiMarko wants to keep your name from being linked with his, Mr. Trent, so he has a suggestion about your end of the story."

Harrison waited.

"The cops are looking for Ms. Bellman

because they know she was at your bachelor party when you disappeared. The woman who runs the temp agency that Mr. Van Wheeler hired told the cops she's a friend of Carolyn Carillo's. She told them she asked Ms. Bellman to fill in as a bartender when she came up short that night."

Jamie made a soft sound that could have been assent or disquiet.

"Mr. DiMarko suggests you claim you had second thoughts about your wedding and you and Ms. Bellman ran off together that night and you've been shacked up here ever since."

Jamie shook her head. "No. For one thing I used my credit card to take a motel room the other night."

"No problem. The two of you went there first, then you suggested this place because it's quieter and unoccupied since Mr. DiMarko bought this house as a retirement gift for the Carillos."

"What!"

"That can be checked," Harrison told him.

"Yes, sir, and county records will substantiate the story."

Jamie protested. "You can't do that! They never owned a place like this."

"I can only tell you what Mr. DiMarko says. The deed is registered in their names, and since you're their heir, the house belongs to you now." He placed two sets of house keys in front of him on the table along with a sheet of paper. "This is the security firm that monitors the place and the alarm sequence. You'll want to have that changed since a number of people have the code."

Jamie gaped at him. "This is a joke."

"No, ma'am."

"Is there anything Mr. DiMarko didn't think of?" she demanded with gritty sarcasm.

"Yes, ma'am. He can't explain away what happened at the Van Wheeler estate. He suggests you tell the police everything was fine when the two of you left in something of a hurry. You'll have to finesse the details, since

Mr. Trent left all his stuff behind. Just keep the explanations short and simple, stick to the truth as much as possible, and deny any knowledge of the events that happened there after you left."

Jamie's expression was blank, but Harrison nodded. "It might work."

"No! Walking out the night before your wedding makes you look like a snake."

Her vehemence made him want to smile. "I'm more concerned about your reputation."

"I can deal," she told him coldly.

"So can I."

"What about Zoe?"

"She'll understand."

"Really? Because I sure wouldn't."

Frank cleared his throat. "Your rental car should be here in a few minutes. You want me to make some breakfast while you two get ready?"

"I'm not hungry."

"You don't have to, Frank," Harrison replied at the same time. "I'm going take a shower and shave now that we don't have to rush out of here."

"Did this house really belong to Tony and Carolyn?" Jamie demanded.

"If Mr. DiMarko says they owned it, they owned it. I'm just the messenger."

Harrison headed upstairs to the bathroom. His father had outdone himself on several levels. With the price of this house, Jamie could easily finance her dream. And maybe Harrison could convince her that they had excellent colleges here in Virginia. All that was left was to find a way to keep Kirsten Parsons alive.

JAMIE WAS STILL STEWING as they drove back into town a while later. Harrison had called Carter and arranged for them to meet the lawyer at his D.C. office. The day was muggy and traffic was heavy. The air conditioner in the rental car struggled and was failing miserably. It was a relief to take their ticket from the machine and pull into the parking garage adjacent to the office building.

The garage was nearly full. They had to park on the upper deck in full sun, which would no doubt be the final straw for the poor air conditioner when they finally returned, but they'd trade the car in as soon as they were finished. Street crews were doing repair work below using pneumatic drills, sending dust billowing into the still air.

"You have to love D.C. in the summer," Harrison murmured as they headed toward the elevator and stairs.

"Speak for yourself. Do you really think we're going to pull this off without getting arrested?"

"Trust me."

She rolled her eyes as a small coupe passed them on its way to one of the few remaining parking spaces. Two women and an older man with a cane exited the stairwell. Jamie's gaze swept the garage nervously.

"We'll lay everything out for Carter and follow his lead."

Even as she listened to Harrison's words, she assessed and dismissed any possible threat from the trio they were approaching. A part of her mind paid attention to every detail around them. Subconsciously, she realized the coupe that had passed them had braked abruptly. There were no parking spaces that close to where they were walking, so she turned.

Kirsten Parsons ran at them, revolver in hand.

"Harrison!" Jamie had time to utter his name in warning an instant before Kirsten pulled the trigger. The sound was muffled by the pneumatic drill, but the bullet came so close to her face, Jamie felt the passage of displaced air. Her hand desperately clawed for the weapons she no longer carried as Kirsten continued running at them. Harrison shoved Jamie aside and went down as Kirsten fired again.

Someone screamed.

Kirsten swung her head in that direction. Jamie flew at her. Kirsten brought the gun around to fire a second too late and they crashed together. Jamie gripped Kirsten's gun hand and they grappled for control. The weapon suddenly discharged twice in rapid succession, muffled by the press of their bodies. Kirsten went slack. Jamie wrenched the gun from her fingers and stepped back. Kirsten folded to the cement floor without a sound. Blood pooled beneath her.

"Are you all right?"

Jamie stared blankly at the older man who appeared beside her. He bent stiffly and felt for a pulse at Kirsten's neck. Shaking his head, he used his cane to stand once more. "You're hurt. Sit down. My daughter called the police. Why don't you give me the gun?"

Her gaze landed on Harrison. He lay unmoving, the side of his head bathed in blood. She ran to him, panic rising inside to consume her. Dimly she heard someone sobbing only to realize the sound was coming from her own throat. "Don't die. Don't you dare die on me!"

ARTIE'S VOICE PULLED HARRISON from the comforting cobweb of haze. "Jamie, you can't keep sitting here."

"I'm not leaving."

"Ms. Bellman, I'm going to have to call security."

This was an unknown voice, stern and gruffly feminine.

"Go ahead. I'm not leaving."

Harrison had to smile at the stubbornness in her voice.

"Let me handle this, all right, nurse?" Artie asked.

Nurse?

"He's got a hard head, Jamie." Artie's voice was inexplicably gentle. "The bullet bounced right off."

Bullet?

"I'm not leaving him." Her voice sounded thick and scratchy as if she'd been crying. "I won't lose him, too."

"You love him."

"He's an idiot. I'm the bodyguard. He had no right to throw himself in harm's way like that. He's stubborn and maddening and *rich!*"

She loved him!

"And you love him," Artie was repeating.

"Yes."

Harrison felt her breath on his ear as she whispered, "I love you so much. Please wake up, Harrison. Don't leave me."

"Not going anywhere." The soft croak hurt his throat. He was so thirsty. He tried to moisten parched lips.

"Harrison?" Something wet splashed against his cheek. "Open your eyes. Look at me."

That was his G.I. Jamie. Full of orders. It was hard, lifting his eyelids, but her face slowly came into focus. "Crying?"

Her lips were soft against his. More tears splashed on his skin.

"You're almost more trouble than you're worth, you know that?"

"Worth a lot."

"I know that, fool."

And then there were strangers in white elbowing her aside, asking stupid questions and shining bright lights in his eyes. Jamie hovered nearby. He sensed her presence even though he couldn't see her anymore. He was so tired and his head hurt abominably. But she loved him. Everything was going to be fine now.

"TELL ME AGAIN why this couldn't wait," Jamie demanded in a cross whisper. Already the hot Florida sun had forced her to demand refuge inside the cabin of the gently rocking boat before the heat could take a toll on Harrison. "You shouldn't even be out of the hospital. You're going to scare her."

"You don't know Zoe."

"Well, you're scaring these people." The nice-looking couple stood on the deck near the opening to the cabin. They were talking together in low voices.

"I don't think I'm the one intimidating them."

"I only asked them for some shade and some water. We don't need you passing out."

He smiled at her and touched her face lightly. "I like the way you fuss over me."

"I do not fuss over you."

The couple moved away to greet someone else. The boat bobbed and seconds later another couple descended the three steps and entered the cabin. Petite and lovely, the woman looked past Jamie to Harrison. Shock widened her eyes. "What did you do? You look awful!"

"Told you so," Jamie whispered, standing quickly and moving aside as far as the confines of the space would allow. Harrison stood to catch the woman, who ran to hug him fiercely.

Jamie moved to stand beside the woman's ruggedly handsome companion. "You must be Xavier Drake. I'm Jamie Bellman."

His wary gaze met hers. "Hello."

"Mark Ramsey told us about you and Zoe."

"Really? He didn't tell us a thing about you."

"That's probably because he didn't expect Harrison to leave the hospital so soon and charter a jet to get us here."

Xavier Drake's expression turned bleak as he

eyed the couple. Zoe was berating Harrison, who was smiling fondly at her.

"They make a good-looking couple, don't they?" Jamie hated the wistful tone in her voice.

Xavier's eyes narrowed. "No. He's too tall and he's bald."

She smiled. "The bald part's temporary. The hospital had to shave part of his head to treat the bullet wound, so he had Artie help him shave the rest to match. It will grow back."

"Shot!" Zoe was exclaiming. "You need a keeper."

"I have one," Harrison told her softly. He captured Jamie's gaze warmly. "Zoe, meet Jamie Bellman."

Zoe turned and studied Jamie's battered cheek, the bandage on her arm where one of Kirsten's bullets had taken skin and the angry scars that circled her wrists. "You're a bodyguard?"

Jamie shrugged. "I'm better when the body in question doesn't deliberately step in the line of fire to protect me."

"That's Harrison," Zoe agreed with a smile. She gestured to the other man. "This is Xavier Drake. He's a pretty good bodyguard, too."

Drake? As in the same last name as Zoe's late ex? Jamie looked at Xavier with new interest. There was probably a lot more to this story than even she and Harrison knew. "I thought Mark Ramsey said you ran the family boat tour business."

"I do."

Zoe grinned impudently.

Harrison proffered his hand. "Harrison Trent. Thanks for looking after her. Zoe means a lot to me."

Drake's jaw tightened. He stared at Harrison as the men shook hands. "She means a lot to me, too."

"Good."

Harrison stepped back. Jamie relaxed when she saw the way his eyes twinkled. "Does this mean our wedding's off?" he asked Zoe lightly.

"You had your chance," she told him with answering good humor. "And you blew it."

His gaze clouded. "I know. I'm sorry, Zoe."

She shook her head. "I'm not. I love you, Harrison. I'll always love you. But I think we both knew we were getting married for the wrong reason."

Relief, sudden and overwhelming, coursed through Jamie. It was going to be all right.

Xavier nudged her. "Want to come topside and stare at the water with me while they get unengaged?"

"Absolutely."

Harrison regarded her with a tender expression. Zoe smiled and winked at Jamie.

Harrison was right. She was going to like Zoe.

* * * * *

millsandboon.co.uk Community

Join Us!

The Community is the perfect place to meet and chat to kindred spirits who love books and reading as much as you do, but it's also the place to:

- **Get the inside scoop from authors about their latest books**
- **Learn how to write a romance book with advice from our editors**
- **Help us to continue publishing the best in women's fiction**
- **Share your thoughts on the books we publish**
- **Befriend other users**

Forums: Interact with each other as well as authors, editors and a whole host of other users worldwide.

Blogs: Every registered community member has their own blog to tell the world what they're up to and what's on their mind.

Book Challenge: We're aiming to read 5,000 books and have joined forces with The Reading Agency in our inaugural Book Challenge.

Profile Page: Showcase yourself and keep a record of your recent community activity.

Social Networking: We've added buttons at the end of every post to share via digg, Facebook, Google, Yahoo, technorati and de.licio.us.

www.millsandboon.co.uk